FOOTBALL SPIRIT

GERARD SIGGINS

THE O'BRIEN PRESS
DUBLIN

First published 2021 by
The O'Brien Press Ltd,
12 Terenure Road East, Rathgar,
Dublin 6, Ireland
D06 HD27
Tel: +353 1 4923333; Fax: +353 1 4922777
E-mail: books@obrien.ie
Website: obrien.ie
The O'Brien Press is a member of Publishing Ireland.

ISBN: 978-1-78849-235-5

8 7 6 5 4 3 2 1
25 24 23 22 21

Printed and bound by Norhaven Paperback A/S, Denmark.
The paper in this book is produced using pulp from managed forests.

Published in

DUBLIN
UNESCO
City of Literature

DEDICATION

To my uncle, David Siggins, the best footballer in the family – ever!

ACKNOWLEDGEMENTS

I first came across the story of Liam Whelan when my dad showed me his grave in Glasnevin Cemetery. Liam – or Billy as they called him in Manchester – was a tantalising story of what could have been, and it is an honour to bring it to you.

This is the ninth Eoin Madden adventure, and his first involving football. Thanks to my brilliant editor Helen Carr for helping me bring him to life once again.

And thanks of course to Martha, Jack, Lucy and Billy for all their support, and to Mam and Dad for everything.

Hope you've found a good spot on the eternal terraces, Dad, with a perfect view of every game you ever want to see.

CHAPTER 1

'So, what do you think about this Transistor Year?' asked Dixie.

'It's *Transition* Year,' replied Eoin with a chuckle. He was never quite sure when his grandfather was being serious. 'It's what we do in school after the Junior Cert. We have a year with only a few lessons and lots of activities – canoeing, hill walking and the like. It should be fun.'

'Fun?' replied the old man. 'When I was a youngster, we had one day off for the school tour, when they brought us to the zoo, or a factory. The rest of the time we were stuck into our books.'

'Well, I suppose of lot of what we do will be educational,' replied Eoin. 'We'll be learning useful skills and things that will help us decide on a career. We could learn how to be a coach, or how to cook, or even learn how to dance.'

Dixie cracked a thin smile. 'Dancing? Ah, now listen, Eoin. That's the stuff you do on a Saturday night when you're older, not on a Monday morning when you would be better off doing double Maths.'

Eoin laughed while he carried his cup over to the sink.

'Thanks for the tea, Grandad; I better get back to my packing.'

'Ah, last-minute Larry, like your father,' chuckled the old man, as he followed Eoin out to the front door. 'Here's something for a few sweets, or a new rugby jersey,' he added as he tucked a fifty euro note into the back pocket of Eoin's jeans.

'Thanks, Grandad,' Eoin replied. 'I got plenty of new rugby shirts this summer, though — maybe I'll put that towards a pair of shiny dancing shoes!'

The old man's mouth opened wide, but he was left speechless — and now it was Eoin's turn to laugh as he set off at jogging pace to his home on the other side of Ormondstown.

He called into his friend Dylan's house to make arrangements for the trip to Dublin. Eoin's dad had offered to drive them up to the city, but the boys decided they would make the day into a bit of an adventure and travel on their own.

'Don't be late for the bus, Dyl,' Eoin stressed to his pal. 'We'll be waiting two hours for the next one – and that will play havoc with your planned trip to that Alabama Fried Chicken place.'

'I'll be here, don't worry. Just trying to pack all I can carry rather than all I will need. I'm starting to have second thoughts about turning down that lift.'

Eoin laughed. 'Well, we don't have to worry about hauling our rugby gear along. They never pick TY boys for the senior panel.'

'Maybe,' replied Dylan. 'But they never had a British and Irish Lions star to pick before.'

CHAPTER 2

Eoin raced home, where his mother was waiting for him with a suitcase, tightly packed and wrapped around with a leather belt. Luckily, he had brought up most of his stuff before the term had started.

'Ah, Mam, you didn't have to do that. Are you sure you have packed everything that I left out to bring?'

'I have of course,' she said with a smile. 'I even remembered that you won't be playing rugby.' She pointed to the small pile of kitbags in the corner. 'We'll have to sort out what you want to keep when you get home next.'

Eoin was actually relieved to be giving rugby a break. He had been very busy last year and playing for Ireland and Leinster as well as Castlerock College pushed him to breaking point. He'd spent the first half of the summer in New Zealand with the Lion Cubs so it was a relief to wind down with his pals playing hurling.

And by the time it came to go back to school he still

wasn't missing rugby.

He was able to cope with the physical side – although some of those hits he took in New Zealand had rattled his bones – but he had always been uncomfortable with the attention that came with being the star. Playing out-half meant he was always the focus of both opponents and his own team, but the better he got as a player the more attention he got off the field too. At first he enjoyed the way the first-year kids would ask him for his autograph, or point him out in the queue for the canteen, but now he hated it.

The past few months had seen his name appearing on both the front and back pages of the newspapers. But averting a disaster in both the Aviva Stadium *and* Croke Park, and becoming a match-winner on both sides of the world would only bring more attention on his shoulders. He was really keen to have a quiet, anonymous Transition Year.

He sorted through his pile of kit, putting aside those he wanted to keep as souvenirs and those he would pass on to the charity shop. The local branch sent on sports shirts to countries in the developing world, and it made him smile to think of a kid in Africa or somewhere playing football wearing his Leinster or Castlerock shirts.

He kept the Ireland ones though, and the beautiful

all-black shirt he had swapped for a Lion Cubs No.10 down in New Zealand. He knew that someday he would have that put in a frame.

He took one of the kit bags and selected a couple of pairs of runners for his regular jogs around the school grounds. He tossed in a couple of shirts and pairs of shorts too, and as he went to zip up the holdall, he stopped and reached for a pair of boots.

'Who knows, I might fancy a run out at some stage,' he said to himself. 'Better to have these to hand than have to borrow a pair.'

And so, packing completed, he wandered downstairs to say goodbye to his parents.

CHAPTER 3

Eoin's dad dropped him down to the bus-stop where there were just a couple of people waiting. They chatted for a minute or two and Mr Madden took a couple of banknotes from his wallet.

'That should keep you in chocolate for a few weeks,' he said with a grin. 'Though I suppose you probably have hundreds of euro stashed away after your summer job.'

Eoin returned the grin. 'No chocolate for me. I'm keeping that for a rainy day. Might be a nice school tour this year.'

They were making their farewells just as the bus came around the bend. Racing alongside it was Dylan, with a small suitcase under one arm and a huge gear bag over the other shoulder.

'Tell him to wait,' his friend roared, as he dropped the case.

Eoin was slow getting on board the coach, allowing Dylan just enough time to catch up and make it up the steps before the doors wheezed shut.

Having paid the driver, Dylan slumped down beside Eoin still struggling to recapture his breath.

'Sorry… 'bout that…' he gasped. 'Mam was… ironing…'

'You're grand, don't worry,' Eoin replied. 'Sure, we're here now and on the way.'

Time flew by for the boys as the bus sped through the midlands towards Dublin. The bus stopped in Portlaoise and among the new passengers was Ross Finnegan, a sixth year in Castlerock.

'Hey there, Madden,' he called out as he inched down the aisle. 'Any spare seats?'

Eoin directed him to one, three seats behind him. Once Ross got settled, he came up to see his schoolmates.

'Fair play to you,' he started. 'That was some display down in New Zealand. We were watching the games on the streaming.'

Eoin shrugged. 'Yeah, cheers,' he replied.

'You're in TY now?' he said. 'I doubt they'll pick you for the senior squad though. We've never had a fourth year on the seniors since Dixie Madden.'

Eoin's grandfather had been a star rugby player at their school and could have played for Ireland.

'Yeah, I reckoned that,' Eoin replied. 'But I'm happy enough taking a year out of rugby and grow a few inches before I start playing against lads your size.'

'Yeah, you are a bit on the small side, I suppose,' Ross replied with a grin as he towered above Eoin. 'And you won't get much bigger on the food they feed us up in Castlerock.'

'I played a bit of GAA over the summer,' said Eoin. 'Do you think they'd let us get a team together?'

'I doubt it,' said Ross. 'They really have a downer on that in Castlerock. They'd even let you play soccer ahead of Gaelic.'

Ross went back to his seat and Eoin closed his eyes, his mind wandering back to his exciting summer and the drama of revisiting Bloody Sunday in Croke Park. School would almost seem like a break after all that, he thought.

CHAPTER 4

Eoin enjoyed the less demanding schedule of Transition Year. There were loads of new subjects, such as design, cookery and engineering, as well as the usual stuff he had been doing since he was five years old. But without a major exam at the end of the year he could enjoy learning for its own sake.

And there was lots of outdoor, active stuff. They were all signed up for a yoga session for the first period every Monday, and Eoin found it extremely useful in understanding how his muscles worked and he found he was starting to become more flexible – which would be useful when he finally returned to rugby.

That first evening back the classmates all met up in the dining hall and filled each other in on their summer activities. Everyone had followed Eoin's adventures in New Zealand so he was happy not to have too many questions about the tour.

'Those Kiwis looked very tough,' said Charlie Bermingham.

Eoin shrugged. 'They're big lads, right enough – but there were a few big lads on the Carrick team we played in hurling later in the summer too.'

There were some new faces in the year, and Eoin and Alan invited them to join them. Sam was from England so he had to have hurling explained to him, and Ernesto was from Uruguay in South America.

'Do you know Lionel Messi?' asked Ferdia, getting his geography very wrong.

The boys were very enthusiastic about the school programme for the year ahead. There was a good mix of activities and academic work – Eoin was really keen on learning a bit about Ancient Greece and Rome – but the range of new sports was what got the boys talking.

Later, as Eoin and Alan went for a walk around the school grounds, he mentioned his decision to take a year out of rugby which left Alan a little dismayed.

'Ah no, Eoin, you can't just give up rugby,' he told him.

'I'm not giving it up,' Eoin replied. 'I just want to take a break – everyone else in the year is getting a break from the boring day to day of school. Why can't I? And anyway they never pick TY lads on the Senior Cup team. Especially scrawny little ones.'

'But… but you're the best player we've had in the school *EVER* – well, at least since Dixie.'

'That's rubbish, Alan, and you know it. I'm still a kid and rugby's a lot harder and tougher when you get to the SCT.'

'Can't you just keep up training with them?'

'No. I want to take a break – with the tours and everything I've been playing non-stop for about two years. If I'm as good as you think I am I'll be able to take it up again, surely.'

Alan frowned. 'But…'

Eoin grinned back at him as they crossed the road towards the area known as The Rock. 'I know what you're thinking. You've worked out loads of great tactics and moves for me and have no one to try them out on?'

Alan smiled back. A keen analyst of rugby, he had indeed been spending a lot of time coming up with various manoeuvres Eoin could experiment with during matches. One or two had proved highly successful.

'Well, you had no complaints when I won that Lions series for you – and the Four Nations,' Alan replied.

Eoin laughed. 'Ah, now Alan, you've got to be joking. I'm grateful for that song you wrote, and working out what we had to do in the last match of the Four Nations, but you can't say you 'won' those things for me.'

Alan grinned, and shrugged his shoulders. 'It's just I'm going to miss the rugby, especially after doing a course on it over the summer.'

They pulled aside the bushes to get through to the quietest part of the school grounds, where Eoin often went for some peace.

'Well, nobody's stopping you staying involved in rugby – but how are you on soccer?' asked Eoin. 'I'm thinking of giving that a go if they won't let me start a Gaelic team. I'd say I could easily find ten or fifteen lads who'd be up for playing a few games.'

CHAPTER 5

Eoin leaned back against the Rock, a huge boulder beside the stream that ran along the outer wall of Castlerock College.

'It is good to be back in this old place, though, isn't it?' he said to Alan.

'I suppose so, but it's a bit of weird year without *proper* classes. Yoga's a bit of crack, and I've asked can I do a rugby coaching course as part of my program.'

'Nice one, they'll probably have you back here as a teacher when you're finished Uni so,' Eoin said with a grin.

'Dylan looks a bit uncomfortable with playing basketball,' said Alan with a grin, 'I don't think he's quite built for it.'

'Alright, take it easy, just because *you* grew four centimetres over the summer. Dylan will always be a titch, he's nearly the same height as his mother.'

'Maybe I could give him a lift, like a line-out jumper?' wondered Alan.

Eoin closed his eyes and lay back on the rock, enjoying a moment's rest in a busy day. He was almost instantly interrupted by Alan.

'Ah, Brian, you gave me a fright,' Alan said. 'Though, I suppose that *is* what ghosts are supposed to do.'

Eoin opened his eyes and jumped off the rock, delighted at the arrival.

'Brian!' he called, 'I haven't seen you since the day of the final in Croke Park. Where have you been?'

'Oh, around and about,' the new arrival replied. 'I was down at Lansdowne Road for a while, checking out the workmen fixing up the stadium. And then I came out here to see what was happening.'

'And found nothing much I suppose?' said Alan, with a grin.

'I'm not sure about that,' said Brian, who was the ghost of a rugby player who died after being injured playing in Lansdowne Road almost a hundred years ago. He had proved to be a great friend to Eoin over several years in school, especially for giving him sound advice about rugby.

'There seems a bit of a buzz around the place,' Brian added. 'I heard a couple of people talking about you and the Lions…'

Eoin blushed. 'Ah, it wasn't really the Lions – they called them the Cubs. But yeah, it was a bit of a laugh.'

Brian frowned. 'Well, I'm not sure there will be much laughing. I only ever seem to appear when there's trouble brewing, not that I'm much able to help. Just be careful lads – and keep your eye out for anything that's a bit different.'

'Different?' asked Alan. 'Sure, everything is different this year – we're doing classes in basketball, cooking and yoga. How different can you get?'

Brian looked puzzled, and Eoin laughed before explaining what happened in Transition Year in schools these days.

Brian looked even more puzzled when he finished talking.

'And they call that *school*?' he asked. 'My old school's idea of a break from the books was Thursday morning when we had a half hour run around the rugby field, no matter what the weather.'

The boys' eyes widened.

'Are you lads out for a run too?'

'No,' replied Eoin, 'we're just having a leisurely stroll. I'm giving up the rugby this year so I won't have to punish myself with the long runs for a while.'

'I'm sorry to hear that,' said Brian. 'You are an excellent player – why are you stopping?'

'I'm just tired of it, Brian,' Eoin replied. 'I've been at it non-stop for about two years and want to try something new. I had great crack with the GAA in the summer so I think I'll get a soccer team going.'

'Soccer?' said Brian. 'I don't think they've ever had a football team in Castlerock before. I can't imagine Andy Finn would be best pleased.'

CHAPTER 6

Eoin and Alan chatted about football on their way back to school. Alan supported Bohemians in the League of Ireland and the English club Leeds United, but Eoin had no personal favourites.

'I never really saw the point of it to be honest,' he said. 'Like, I support Tipp in hurling, and Munster in rugby, because that's where I'm from. But there's no big football team near me – so I certainly am not going to pick a team in England or Spain just for the sake of it.'

Alan nodded. 'Yeah, good point. I only support my teams because my grandfather did – I've never been to see them play, but I check their scores every week. Does that count as being a supporter?'

'Well, I suppose it does in a way, but not a very good one. Maybe you could send off for a black and red Bohs beanie instead of that smelly Leinster one you always wear,' he replied with a laugh.

They discussed an Ireland game that Eoin had watched on television the week before, and they agreed they would go along next time there was a big match.

'A few of the guys are big into football – they're always in the common room on Sundays watching matches. Kevin, Charlie, John Young, Figo. Maybe Theo and Benjy too. We'll ask around and see if there's any interest in playing a bit.'

As they reached the school they met Dylan wearing a basketball singlet and baggy shorts.

'Howya, Dyl,' said Alan. 'Shoot any baskets?'

Dylan scowled back at him. 'Very funny,' he said. 'This game is brilliant except for the fact you have to be a giant to score. But I love the skills of it, running with the ball and all that. I'll be fine when I grow an extra six inches.'

Alan and Eoin looked at each other, but decided it was better not to comment.

'Do you fancy getting involved in soccer?' Eoin asked. 'I'm serious about it now, I'm going to ask the headmaster as soon as I have enough players to play a few seven-a-sides among ourselves. Who knows, there might be another school near us who'd give us a game later on in the year.'

'I love the soccer,' said Dylan, 'and I'm good at it too.

And I bet I'm the only one here who's been to a League of Ireland match.'

Alan and Eoin shuffled their feet and looked sheepish.

'Right so, I'll play if you make me the captain,' said Dylan. 'And I get to pick the team too.'

'Hang on, hang on,' said Eoin. 'I've just set up this team and you've already taken it over. I've no problem with you being captain if you want to – I don't think it's that big a deal in football anyway. But it can't be a one-man show. The three of us will pick the team, if it even comes to that. We mightn't get enough players in TY.'

'Ah, we will, no doubt. I'll get the word around if you square it with old McCaffrey.'

Eoin decided to grab the bull by the horns and called into the main school building. He knocked on the office door and the secretary beckoned him into the room.

'Hello, Eoin, you've been busy since I saw you last,' she said with a smile. 'The headmaster is ready now, so head in. You know the way.'

Mr McCaffrey was just as delighted to see Eoin and asked him lots of questions about his summer adventures, and especially about New Zealand.

'The rugby was tough,' admitted Eoin, 'but we got to

see a fair bit of the country and it really is as beautiful as they say.'

Mr McCaffrey smiled. 'But now, of course, you didn't come in here to tell me all about your holidays. Is there anything I can help you with?'

Eoin started: 'Well, I had an idea I just wanted to run past you...'

'Go on,' said the headmaster.

'Well, you know I'm in Transition Year, and how there's never anyone in TY on the Senior Cup panel? I was talking to a few of my pals and we thought we'd give rugby a miss this year and maybe set up a football team instead. Just to keep up the fitness for next year, of course.'

Mr McCaffrey's jaw dropped open, and his cheeks started darkening.

'Oh no, no, no. That won't do at all. We've *never* had a... a *soccer* team in Castlerock. And just because you won't be playing on the SCT this year doesn't mean rugby just stops. Mr Carey and Andy Finn are very keen on the TY boys continuing the momentum – there'll be plenty of friendly games and some sort of mini-league competition too.'

Eoin frowned. 'Well, I'd prefer not to keep playing this year, sir. I've been playing for two years solid with lots of games in the summer too and I want to take a break. This seems like the obvious year to do it and then come back refreshed for the Senior Cup.'

Mr McCaffrey stood and walked to the window. He stared out towards the playing fields for a minute and then turned back.

'Eoin,' he started. 'I want you to go away and think what winning the Senior Cup two years from now would mean to you, and to the school,' he said. 'Giving up rugby for a year presents a real danger that you might never get back in the groove again when you return. And, of course, there's always the chance of injury playing other sports.'

Eoin knew there was much less chance of being injured playing football than rugby, but he decided not to interrupt the head.

McCaffrey went on, 'I'll have a word with the coaches and see if they can give you a few weeks off rugby because of your activity in the summer. But there will be *no* talk of giving up the game.'

CHAPTER 7

Eoin was a bit stunned after his meeting with Mr McCaffrey. And more than a little annoyed too. He kicked a pencil someone had dropped and muttered, 'It's supposed to be a free country,' to himself as he headed back to the dormitories.

He also tried to remember what exactly the headmaster had said about football. Mr McCaffrey was so shocked by the idea of the school's best player in fifty years quitting that he had brushed over the talk of a soccer team.

'He only said there had never been a school football team in the past,' Eoin said to himself, 'not that there wasn't to be one in the future.'

Eoin decided that he would see what sort of reception he got from the rest of the boys before he made any rash moves.

When he got to their room Dylan and Alan were

lying on their beds discussing football.

'I'm a Man U man, Alan, we're used to winning trophies, unlike your crowd, *Leeds*,' Dylan said, pronouncing the last word as if it made an unpleasant smell when he spoke it.

'Well at least Dyl has watched Man U on the telly, Alan,' agreed Eoin.

'I did see Leeds on telly once,' Alan protested. 'They beat Man U actually.'

That kept Dylan quiet for a few seconds, allowing Eoin to tell them what had happened in the headmaster's office.

'He can't do that – can he?' fumed Dylan.

'I suppose he can make it difficult if I give up rugby…' answered Eoin.

'But you could make it more awkward for him if you gave it up completely. That would make the newspapers!' replied Alan.

'That's a good point, Al,' said Dylan. 'Just say you're giving up rugby for good.'

'But hang on,' said Eoin, 'I *enjoy* playing rugby – I don't want to give it up, just to take a break.'

'Well, McCaffrey says he'll talk to the coaches about giving you a few weeks off,' said Alan. 'We'll get the football going and see how that goes. You might be happy to go back to the rugby then.'

Eoin thought about it for a moment.

'You know something, that just might work. There's a bit of breathing space there. Maybe they'll have forgotten me by then on the SCT too.'

Eoin relaxed, enjoying the solution and that breathing space, but it wasn't for long as a knock came to their door.

'Madden, can I have a word?' said Mr Carey, one of the teachers who also coached rugby.

Eoin stepped out into the corridor.

'I've just been with the headmaster and I've come straight here,' said Mr Carey, who was clearly annoyed. 'What's this nonsense about you giving up rugby?'

Eoin explained his need for a break, but Mr Carey was having nothing of it.

'What do you mean, *a breather*? We are planning the senior cup campaign for the next three years and we see you playing a major role in all three years. You may not wear the No.10 this year, but I want you around the squad learning how we do things and stepping up if required. So, there is no room for a breather I'm afraid.

'Training starts on Wednesday, straight after school.'

CHAPTER 8

oin was stunned. His room-mates could see from his face just how the meeting had gone.

'Ah no, that's so unfair. After all you did for this school,' said Alan, when Eoin had told them what Mr Carey had ordered.

'I don't even have any gear,' complained Eoin. 'I'll have to get Dad to send it up by courier.'

Dylan stood up and put his hand on Eoin's shoulder.

'I'm still going to go ahead with getting the football team together. You're welcome to come along and join in anytime.'

Eoin grinned. 'Thanks Dyl, you make your takeover sound like you're doing me a favour.'

To be fair to Dylan, he went about forming a soccer club with gusto. His first move was an advertisement pinned to the common room noticeboard.

CASTLEROCK FC
A FOOTBALL (soccer) CLUB is being fromed
for TY students.
CONTACT DYLAN COONAN.
No messers

The notice created quite a stir and Dylan had several boys come up to him to ask to be included.

'What do you think, lads?' he asked Alan and Eoin when they joined him in the common room to watch some TV after dinner.

'Pretty impressive,' said Eoin.

'Fair play, Dyl,' said Alan, 'and it would have been even more impressive if you'd spelt "formed" correctly.'

Dylan made a correction to the poster, growling at Alan as he did so.

'Are you guys here to watch the match?' asked one of the fifth years. 'It's just we need a majority to decide which game to watch. These lads want Chelsea, but if you vote our way, we can watch Manchester United – it's a Champions League game.'

'No doubt,' said Dylan, 'and these two will do what I tell them. In football anyway.'

The boys joined the large group watching the football. It was the first game Eoin had watched in quite a while, so he kept quiet and just studied the action.

Dylan, on the other hand, was quite animated by the play and every time United got near the German team's goal he leapt out of his seat and urged on his team.

At the back of the group of boys watching the game sat Alan and Eoin.

'What position do you play, Eoin?' whispered Alan.

'I don't know,' Eoin replied. 'I haven't really played much since we had a little club in primary school. I suppose I could play central midfield, directing the play – it's a bit like being out-half isn't it?'

Alan nodded. 'I must see if there's a book on football tactics in the library. It seems like a very simple game, but I'd like to study this a bit more.'

'Are you going to volunteer to be the coach?' asked Eoin.

'I doubt if Dylan will let me share his power,' replied Alan with a grin. 'But I might come up with a few ideas that would help.'

They were interrupted by a loud cheer as the Red Devils scored the first goal of the game. Dylan took off like a hare, whooping and hollering around the room and swinging his school jersey.

'Uni-TED, Uni-TED,' he roared, just as one of the teachers came to the door.

'Keep it down in here please, and get back to your seat Mr Coonan,' he snapped. 'Any more roaring and I'll pull the plug.'

That ensured the rest of the game was watched in relative peace, even as United slammed in two more goals to claim full points in the Champions League.

'I think our team should wear red shirts,' said Dylan as they walked back to their sleeping quarters.

Eoin grinned. 'It would be nice to wear the Munster shirt around here, it might give a fright to those Leinster supporters who want me to go their Academy when I'm finished school.'

'But what about lads that don't have Man United or Munster shirts?' asked Alan. 'Lads like me?'

'Everyone has a red shirt, surely?' said Dylan. 'There's lads from Cork who'll play, and there's a load of Liverpool supporters too. But if you're stuck, we could get someone in the laundry room to dye your Leeds shirt red.'

CHAPTER 9

ylan came rushing up to Eoin at the small break next day. He was clutching a copy book and had a big grin on his face.

He started:, 'OK, Eoin, you won't believe it, but I have seventeen lads signed up! Some of them say they've even played the game at a decent level.'

'That's great news, you mightn't need me so.'

'Ah, no way,' said Dylan. 'You have to come out and play for the crack anyway. I'll make sure nobody kicks you.'

'Alright, so who have you got?' asked Eoin.

'Charlie Bermingham's joining – he has a red Liverpool shirt – and the English lad Sam who joined this year.'

Dylan read aloud the rest of the list before stopping at the last name.

'And you'll never guess who's mad keen to join. One

of your oldest pals.'

Eoin scratched his head.

'Chelsea fan?' Dylan hinted.

'Ah no – *Richie Duffy*?' Eoin replied, guessing the name of the boy he had battled with for the No.10 rugby shirt early in his career in Castlerock, and who was the class bully until Eoin successfully stood up to him.

'Full marks, he's supposed to be a good footballer. He hasn't played rugby since second year and he was playing soccer with a club at the weekends. He could be good.'

'So when is the first training session?' asked Eoin.

'We're going to have a run-around for an hour before dinner on Wednesday,' Dylan replied. 'Maybe you could pop along to the junior pitches after rugby training?'

'I suppose I could sneak a red shirt into my rugby bag – in fact, I'll probably have to wear it at rugby training as nothing has arrived from home yet.'

'That's perfect, and by the way, I had a good think and I've decided on the name of our team – we're going to be called the Castlerock Red Rockets.'

Over the next two nights all Eoin heard in the dormitory was Alan and Dylan discussing the Red Rockets and designing a crest for their shirts, if they ever got to that stage of needing one. Alan drew, fairly obviously, a red rocket zooming into the sky, but the background was of a large boulder that was shaped just like the Rock in the school grounds.

'Maybe Brian will come along and support us,' he said.

CHAPTER 10

Wednesday afternoon rolled around and Eoin reluctantly packed a bag with boots, socks, shorts and a rugby shirt. It was strange walking into a changing-room that was so familiar yet completely different.

None of the boys he had been playing with for years were there, although he remembered Danny Tucker and Tim Synnott from when he was called up for the Junior Cup team in second year.

'Hi, Eoin,' called Tim. 'Good to see you in with the big boys. They're not a bad bunch of lads.'

Ross Finnegan, who Eoin had met on the bus to Dublin, walked over to say hello too, with a serious expression.

'Any of these lads gives you any trouble, talk to me,' he told him, before breaking into laughter. 'They'll be fine,' he added. 'We were all talking about you earlier after class – there's a lot of respect for what you've done for Ireland and the Lions, so everyone's delighted to have you on board.'

Eoin smiled and quickly changed into his kit.

'We have special training tops this year,' Tim told Eoin, as he tossed a cellophane packet across the room towards him.

Eoin slipped into the new top, relieved that he didn't have to fish the Munster jersey out of his bag in front of a dressing room packed with Leinster supporters.

Training was not too difficult, Mr Carey easing the boys back in after the summer break. He took Eoin aside for a moment just before the end.

'I'm pleased you decided to come along Eoin, and I hope you're enjoying this. Besides Gavin, you're easily the next-best No.10 in the group so I expect you'll be getting a fair few minutes this season. We'll be upping it to three sessions a week next month so make sure you get your school work done when you can. There won't be much time for anything else.'

Eoin smiled thinly, and thanked Mr Carey.

Once training was over, Eoin grabbed his bag and left promptly, hurrying away to the other side of the school where the first-year rugby pitches were situated.

'Hey lads, hope I'm not too late,' he said, pulling the

training top over his head and easing into the red of his native province.

'Not at all,' said Dylan, 'we're just having a light jog to get the muscles going. You're probably well warmed up anyway.'

Alan, who had decided to sit out the jog, was sitting on a pile of kitbags with his copybook and pen in hand.

'We spent most of the first half hour finding out what position people play, and what clubs they support in England,' he whispered. 'It was a bit of a waste of time, really. Dylan's not a great organiser.'

'Well, be fair to him, he organised a good bunch to come along here,' said Eoin. 'But I agree, he's getting tied up in silly details when he needs to get them enjoying themselves so they will all come back next time.'

When the jog was finished, Eoin showed them how to do a few simple stretches and suggested they have a bit of a kick about – there was enough for an eight-a-side game and Charlie had brought along a football.

'Grand so,' said Dylan. 'As we're called the Red Rockets we're all going to need some sort of red shirt for games. But tonight only about half of us have one so we'll all play together and the rest of you make up another team.'

There was a bit of muttering that Dylan seemed to

41

have found himself on the team with some of the better players, but no one had a better idea.

'Will you captain the multi-coloured team, Richie?' Dylan suggested.

'Yeah, no problem,' replied Duffy, who was wearing a brand new Chelsea shirt.

'These goals are the wrong size,' complained Charlie, 'they should be wider and lower.'

'We'll just have to do with them for the moment,' said Dylan. 'And anyway, it's just a mess match.'

It was quickly clear to Eoin that there was a wide range in standard between the best and worst players, but he thought there were easily enough who knew how to play.

Duffy was actually quite a stylish midfielder, although a bit selfish when it came to passing close to goal. Eoin kept away from him – as he did most days in school – but was impressed at how good he was on the ball.

'That's enough, lads, we better head in for the dinner,' said Dylan once the Red team had taken a 5-4 lead.

There was some minor grumbling, but nobody was too concerned, especially as Dylan had already left the field and was taking off his boots on the sideline.

'Well, that went well, didn't it?' said Dylan. 'I think we have the makings of a seriously good side here.'

CHAPTER 11

ylan was buzzing all evening, and he and Alan spent most of dinner time scribbling in a notebook and making formations out of the players that had impressed them.

'Do I get a place in this team?' asked Eoin.

'Yeah...' replied Dylan. 'But we see you more as a defensive midfielder, we'll play Richie just in front of you to make the chances.'

Eoin shrugged. 'Fair enough, I probably won't be available much anyway.'

He told the boys about Mr Carey's conversation but Dylan wasn't as annoyed as he had been after Eoin's earlier chat with the rugby coach.

'Oh well,' he said. 'I suppose we could do without you if we had to.' And he and Alan started reorganising the formation to see how it would look if Eoin wasn't available.

Eoin felt a little lost by all this, and went for a ramble down to the Rock, where he was delighted to meet Brian.

'You look pretty glum, Eoin, is everything alright?' asked his spectral pal.

'I used to love sport, every sport, but now it just causes me headaches. I've been forced to play rugby on a team I don't really want to play on just because I'm better than anyone else in the year. And when I set up my own football team I'm pressured not to play, and when we finally get going my best friends have written me out of the team. Of course I'm "glum"!'

'That's unfortunate,' replied Brian, 'but perhaps you're just tired of sport after that long summer, as you told me last week. Go for a long run on your own, I always found that a great way of improving my mood. And maybe instead of playing a match you should go to watch one, the excitement and fellow feeling with the rest of the spectators will remind you of why you love sport.'

Eoin smiled and told Brian he thought that sounded like a good idea, and that he would try his suggestions. But he was still very down and a little upset that his friends would cast him aside so easily.

'Anything else happening up in the school?' asked Brian.

'All quiet at the moment, I'll let you know if anything changes,' Eoin replied.

Eoin went for a twenty-minute run before he returned to the dormitory.

'Ah there you are, Eoin, we were making plans to go to watch a game on Saturday,' said Dylan. 'I've decided that now we are part of the Irish football pyramid, I need to support a local club, so naturally enough I'm now a fan of Limerick FC, my native city.'

Alan went on, 'And by chance they are playing in Dublin tomorrow night – against my beloved Bohemians!'

'So we were thinking we could head over to watch the game,' said Dylan. 'It's a five o'clock kick off so we'll be back before the gates close. Are you up for it?'

Eoin nodded. He wasn't sure he wanted to listen to the two of them prattling on about the Red Rockets, but thought it would be good to get out and watch a game as Brian had suggested.

'I've worked out all the logistics,' said Alan. 'It's on the other side of the city, but we can get the Number 4 bus pretty much door to door, nice seats in the stand, grab a burger on the way home and we'll be back before eight o'clock. Not a word to anyone else though – it looks like it might be out of bounds.'

'Will we be stuck in the middle of Bohs fans?' asked Dylan.

'Yeah, so you'll have to behave yourself,' said Alan with a chuckle. 'No jumping up and down if, by some fluke, Limerick manage to score.'

CHAPTER 12

The three friends arrived at the bus stop just as the No 4 was pulling in. They paid their fares and clambered on board before heading for the seats at the very back of the top deck.

Alan checked the time on his phone. 'OK, the bus journey should be about forty minutes, then a five minute walk to Dalymount, so we'll have nearly an hour to explore and find the best seats.'

'Has anyone been here before?' asked Eoin.

'My dad pointed it out to me one day when we were driving to the zoo,' explained Alan. 'He suggested we go to see a Bohs match sometime, but we haven't got around to it yet. His dad, my grandfather, used to play a bit for them way back. He passed away when I was really small, but there's some nice pictures of him at home wearing the red and black shirt.'

'I wonder have they got a Handy Stand,' Eoin replied,

with a grin.

'Very funny,' said Alan. 'I don't think he played for very long. But he was really good. Well so Dad said anyway.'

'Your name could come in useful if you ever start writing books about coaching,' said Dylan. 'Like – you could call them *The Handy Guide to Football,* or *The Handy Guide to Rugby.*'

The boys all laughed and settled back to enjoy the scenery. Eoin hadn't seen much of Dublin in his time there, mostly just rugby grounds and other schools. He noticed how the landscape changed a lot through the course of the journey, from big houses with large gardens and tree-lined roads, to the sights of a bustling city and then to smaller homes and apartment blocks.

'We're dead lucky to be going to a place like Castlerock,' he told his friends as they passed a city school. 'I'd say the lads in there would love to have *one* soccer pitch in their grounds, let alone what we have.'

Alan and Dylan nodded, but they perked up when they noticed a group of men wearing black and red scarves walking briskly alongside the bus.

'I *so* have to buy one of them,' said Alan.

'Who are you supporting, Eoin?' asked Dylan. 'Or have you forgotten your Munster roots entirely?'

Eoin laughed, and looked out the window again. 'I

must confess I do like the Bohs shirt – and the Limerick one only reminds me of Chelsea, and Richie Duffy.'

'So Bohs it is,' chuckled Alan. 'They might give us a discount if we buy two scarves.'

But there were no bargains to be had from the souvenir sellers and Eoin reluctantly parted with ten euro for his new team's colours. The boys wandered up a lane between two terraces of houses where they came to the back of the main stand.

They queued at the under-sixteens turnstile and handed over another five euro note for admission.

'This better be good,' Eoin told his pals. 'I won't have much for my burger on the way home at this rate.'

The trio wandered around the stand, soaking in the views of the famous old ground.

'I don't recognise ye, lads,' said an old gentleman sitting in the back row of the stand.

'It's our first game here,' Alan explained.

'Well I'm glad yiz are flying the right colours,' he chuckled, wheezily.

'Are you a Bohs fan too?' Eoin asked.

'I am indeed, for manys a long year too,' replied the old man, who said his name was Alfie. 'I've been coming here since I was seven year old – and that wasn't today or yesterday. I even played a few games for the Gypsies – that's the fans' name for Bohemians – when I was a young man. I wasn't bad, but they had a lot better players than me at the time.'

The old man told them about the days when the ground was packed with more than 50,000 people, the terraces heaving with supporters in what was the main international ground in Ireland from the 1920s up to the 1970s.

'I saw lots of great players here – there was lads standing all along the roof of the stand there when Ireland played Italy and France in the 1980s. I saw the great Paolo Rossi here, and earlier on Pele and Bobby Charlton too.'

Even the boys had heard of the last two legends. Alan asked him what goal was the best he had ever seen at the old ground.

'That's an easy one,' he replied. 'It was by a fella called Johnny Giles – he used to be on the television a lot, talking about football. When he was only eighteen or nineteen he scored with a screamer from outside the penalty box – just over there,' he pointed out the spot. 'Against Sweden it was.

'He was a great player, but he wasn't the best player I

ever saw.'

Alan's eyes opened wide. 'Was that Pele or Bobby Charlton?'

'No,' he replied, 'and I saw Jimmy Greaves too, but no, the best player I ever saw came from just up the road there,' he said, pointing away to his left.

'Who was that?' asked Dylan.

The old man took off his cap and rubbed his hand backwards across his white hair. 'That was a lad called Liam Whelan,' he replied. 'Lived up there in Cabra, and a darling footballer he was too.'

CHAPTER 13

Eoin looked at Alan, but his blank face told him that he hadn't a clue who the old man was talking about either.

'I haven't heard of him, I'm afraid,' Alan admitted.

'Ah, young lads these days have no idea about the history of the sport – and I see one of ye is a Manchester United fan too,' he replied, pointing at Dylan's red shirt. 'You should definitely know all about Liam, one of your club's greatest heroes.'

'How long ago was this?' asked Eoin.

'More than sixty year ago,' said Alfie. 'I saw him play here a couple of times for Ireland – we nearly beat England too, they only equalised in the last minute. I think he only played four games for Ireland in all.

'But no, the one I remember was the game he played here for United against Shamrock Rovers in the European Cup – that was the old name for the Champions

League. The place was jammers. It was a brilliant occasion for the city, and a great honour for Dalymount to host the famous Busby Babes – they were called that because their manager's name was Matt Busby.

'Rovers were our great enemies so I was cheering for United – and because Liam was playing for them of course.'

The old man smiled with a faraway look in his eyes.

'He was just brilliant, he could get the ball past anyone, and he scored two goals that day – United won 6-0. Our Liam Whelan, from Cabra.'

'But if he was that good, why did he only play four times for Ireland?' asked Dylan.

Alfie sighed. 'I'm afraid that's a long story, youngster.

'Only a few months after the game here United were off in foreign parts playing another European match and on the way back they stopped to refuel in Germany – a city called Munich. The weather was bad and the plane crashed taking off.'

'No way,' said Dylan. 'And was anyone hurt?'

'There was more than twenty people killed,' said Alfie, 'players, coaches, journalists... A fellow called Duncan Edwards was killed – they say he could have been the best player in the world. Bobby Charlton was badly injured, but he recovered and went on to win the World

Cup with England.'

'And was Liam Whelan OK?' asked Eoin.

Alfie shook his head and wiped the corner of his eye. The boys remained silent, shocked at the story.

'The whole city of Dublin was in shock, especially around these parts. Liam was such a hero to everyone. And we've never forgotten him either – there's a bridge named in his honour over that way,' he pointed off into the distance.

'And did he ever play for Bohemians?' asked Alan.

'No, he didn't,' replied Alfie. 'He went over to England when he was still a schoolboy so he only played here for Home Farm and a little local team... what were they called... ah yes, they were the Red Rockets.'

The three boys' mouths opened and they turned to stare at each other.

'Did you say, Red Rockets?' asked Alan.

'Yeah, that's what they were called – I played for them myself for a while.'

'That's funny,' said Dylan. 'We've just started a football club in school and that's what we called them too.'

'Well isn't that a coincidence,' said Alfie. 'Old Liam must be looking down on ye and giving you some inspiration. Well I hope you do well with your little team and I see you again in a few years out on that lovely field,' he added, pointing out to where the players were now having a pre-match kickabout.

'I better go off and get a cup of tea,' he said with a smile. 'That's part of my tradition before every match, and I don't want to change it on the back of winning our last three home games.'

'It was very nice to meet you, sir,' Eoin told him.

'Ah, don't be calling me sir,' Alfie replied. 'I'm Alfie to everyone around here. I hope we see you back here again too.' And off he went in search of his hot drink.

Alan exhaled loudly as he leaned back against the back of the stand. 'Well, that was a bit of a shock,' he said.

'I never heard of the Red Rockets before,' said Dylan. 'I just made up the name for our team.'

'Maybe Alfie's right,' Eoin wondered aloud. 'Maybe that Liam Whelan fella is inspiring you in some way, a bit like Brian did with me.'

Since Eoin arrived in Castlerock he had encountered a series of ghosts of famous sportsmen who also made a mark in different ways, such as Irish rebel Kevin Barry and All Blacks legend Dave Gallaher.

Alan scratched his head. 'That's just mad,' he said.

'Brian warned me there was some trouble brewing,'

replied Eoin. 'Maybe this has something to do with it. We'll keep our eyes open. But let's keep the name Red Rockets too – it may be some connection to that Liam lad.'

CHAPTER 14

The game kicked off and the boys were soon lost in the action. Dalymount Park had seen better days, and large areas of the ground were now closed to spectators. But the terrace behind one goal was packed, and there were very few spare seats to be had in the grandstand.

Dylan realised he would have to dampen down his support for Limerick, but Alan and Eoin were pretty subdued too. Having only previously been at rugby matches, they weren't sure whether football supporters shouted and sang the same things, so they waited to pick up the chants from the fans sitting near them.

Bohemians were on the attack for most of the opening half and a powerful strike from outside the box by their young striker Seb Joyce gave them the lead just before the break. Almost everyone in the stand stood up and cheered, confirming for Dylan that he was watching from enemy territory.

Alan winked at his Limerick-supporting pal, who was trying to pretend he was delighted that Bohs had scored.

'That was a great goal, wasn't it, Dyl?' Eoin teased him.

'Not bad, it was the best I've seen this season anyway,' replied Dylan.

The ref whistled for half-time just afterwards and the trio settled down to discuss what they had seen.

'That Limerick central defender is very dirty,' said Alan. 'He's kicked Seb Joyce twice when the ref wasn't looking.'

'Yeah, the ref is letting them away with murder,' said Eoin. 'Bohs should be two or three up by now.'

Dylan wouldn't be drawn to defend his team's player, for fear he would reveal himself to the home fans sitting in front.

Eoin took in the surroundings and the people around him. He wasn't quite nervous, just unsure of himself in a new place where he wasn't sure how to behave.

'Is this your first game?' asked the man seated in the row in front.

'Is it that obvious,' laughed Eoin.

The man smiled back. 'I suppose it is – ye are like church mice at the back there. You should join in with the singing and the chants. How have you become Bohs fans?'

Alan explained how his grandfather had played for the club, but the man and his companion were too young to have heard of him.

'You should ask Alfie about him – he's been around here for donkey's years – he'll remember him right enough.'

'We met Alfie before the game,' replied Alan. 'But I never got a chance to ask him.'

'It's hard to get in a word edgeways with Alfie,' the man replied. 'He was probably telling you all about Liam Whelan, was he?'

'He was!' replied Eoin. 'He seems to have been a great player.'

'Well Alfie says so, and he's a very good judge of foot-ballers.'

The second half was all Bohs, with Joyce completing his hat-trick, although Dylan allowed himself a smile when Limerick picked up a consolation goal towards the end.

'Five-one, that was some value for money,' said Alan as they wandered towards the exits. As they passed the doorway into the club bar, they spotted Alfie.

'Well lads,' he called, 'Did you enjoy your first visit to Dalyer?'

'It was brilliant,' gushed Alan, 'and thanks for explaining so much of the history for us.'

'No problem,' the old man replied. 'It's great to find youngsters happy to listen to me rabbiting on about the good old days.'

'It was really interesting,' Eoin added.

'Do you have a few minutes, lads?' Alfie asked. 'It's just there's some great photos inside here I'd love to show you,' as he pointed to the doorway. 'You won't be let into the bar, but there's a few on the walls just outside it.'

'I suppose so...' said Dylan, checking out that his friends agreed. They followed Alfie inside.

'Here's a photo of the great Manchester United team that played here,' he said, pointing out his hero Liam Whelan.

He showed them a few photos of other great players and told them he'd get them a full tour of the collection if they came early on the next match day.

As they were leaving, Eoin turned back and said, 'Alan forgot to mention that his grandfather used to play here for Bohemians.'

'Really? What was his name, I might remember him?' he asked.

'Handy. Phil Handy,' Alan replied.

The old man's face turned pale.

'Well now,' he started, 'that's a name I haven't heard in many a year. I'll tell you now son, Phil Handy was one of the best players I ever saw in the old red and black. You should be very proud of your grandfather. He could have played for Ireland. And it was a terrible tragedy for this club too that he stopped playing.'

Alfie told them that he had to meet someone so made his farewells and headed towards the bar, but Eoin was sure that he saw a tear escape from the corner of his eye as he turned his head away from them.

CHAPTER 15

The detour with Alfie meant the boys had to dash to make their bus and so missed their planned visit to the burger restaurant.

Dylan wasn't happy.

'I am always grouchy when I'm hungry,' he complained, looking longingly out the bus window as they passed several chip shops and lots of restaurants offering food from almost every nation on earth.

But Alan had a plan. 'Let's get off at the stop after the school and we can go the twenty-four-hour shop there for snacks. Dinner's never any good on a Saturday night so we can stock up for the evening.'

Eoin thought that sounded like a good idea, although he was trying to eat healthier after a summer when he had let his habits slip.

Dylan moaned that they would have a 'much longer' walk back to school, but Alan and Eoin had stopped listening to him by then.

'I wonder what happened to Grandad that he stopped playing,' Alan asked Eoin. 'I'll have to ask Dad next time he calls over.'

'Yeah, it was a bit of a mystery that,' agreed Eoin. 'I wonder was it a bit like Dixie?'

Eoin's grandfather was a very good rugby player who retired just as he was about to become a star, and Eoin spent much of his first year at the school trying to find out why.

The Number 4 sailed past Castlerock and the boys got off at the next stop, thanking the driver as they got off.

Dylan raced to be first in the queue and ordered two large sausage rolls and two bags of crisps.

'How are you going to eat all that?' Eoin asked him, after he chose an energy bar and an apple.

'No trouble to me, I'm starving after all that fresh air,' replied Dylan.

Alan joined Dylan in buying sausage rolls and the trio munched their food as they strolled back to the school.

'So, what did you think of your first soccer match?' asked Dylan between bites.

'Very enjoyable,' replied Alan. 'It was a lot more crack than watching a match on television.'

'Yeah, I thought that too,' said Eoin, 'and it was interesting to watch from up high and see the formations they take and how they change them as the game develops. You could see players running off the ball a lot, which you rarely see on the TV.'

Alan admitted he had been reading a book about football tactics and was interested in coaching the Red Rockets if Dylan thought he could help.

'Well, I was thinking I would fit more of a player-manager role,' replied Dylan, 'but we'd still need a coach to put out the cones and all that.'

'Put out the cones? There's a bit more to it than that,' laughed Alan.

The sun was starting to set when they slipped back into the grounds of Castlerock where they met Mr McCaffrey just outside the main school building.

'Good evening, boys, it's a nice night for a stroll,' the headmaster said. 'I'm afraid you've missed dinner but cook may have some leftovers that would make a sandwich for you. Is that a football scarf I see there – where have you all been?'

Eoin stepped forward: 'We just went to see a football match, sir. Dylan's team from down home were playing so we went along to see them.'

'And did they win?' asked Mr McCaffrey.

'No sir,' replied Dylan. 'They lost 5-1.'

'Well, that must have been very disappointing for you. But do hurry on there, cook will want to be getting home for the evening so you better get to her right away, unless you want to starve.'

The boys arrived just in time and the cook was not too irritated by their late arrival. She made them each a chicken sandwich, which they took up to their room.

As they munched, they discussed what they would do next with the Red Rockets.

'We'll try and train twice a week, and hopefully we'll have enough players to have a few eleven versus eleven games between ourselves,' said Dylan.

'But we should also try to get a few friendlies against other schools?' asked Alan. 'It might be nice to test ourselves.'

'We could see if the lads in Ligouri would give us a game,' suggested Eoin.

'Definitely,' said Dylan, 'but let's see how the next couple of weeks go first.'

CHAPTER 16

There was a nasty surprise waiting for the boys when they got down to the dining hall for breakfast.

They had just collected their food and taken their seats when the headmaster stormed in.

'Coonan, Handy, Madden, come here please,' he thundered, waving a newspaper in the air and directing them to join him at the main entrance.

'When you told me you had gone to see some local team play a football match, I presumed it was some park kickabout, not a professional League of Ireland game on the far side of the city,' he started, pointing to the match report in the newspaper.

Eoin gulped, and thought, *We should never have told him the score.*

Dylan tried to explain. 'But sir, it wasn't that far away at all,' he said, 'we got the bus outside and it left us right at the ground. You saw we got home before dark.'

But Mr McCaffrey was in no mood for explanations. 'I'm sorry, but that ground is far too far away from the school for you to be getting buses to it without express permission. And where has this new interest in soccer come from? I thought you were all keen rugby players?'

'We still are, sir,' Alan explained. 'It's just there's not much rugby for TY students and we thought we'd set up a soccer club – loads of boys are interested in playing. For fitness, like.'

'*Loads?*' replied the headmaster, looking angrier than ever. 'I don't want *loads* of Castlerock boys being distracted away from rugby. Winning the Leinster Schools Senior Cup is most important to this school. Any distraction from that is simply unacceptable. I thought Mr Carey had made that clear to you, Mr Madden.'

Eoin shuffled his feet and stared at the ceiling for a few seconds before he replied.

'I'm playing rugby this year, sir. I won't miss a single training session or game. But I also want to play football with my friends, and that's why we have set up this soccer club.'

Mr McCaffrey stared back at him. 'But you won't have time to do both … and you could get injured…'

'I could get injured playing rugby, sir,' Eoin replied. 'In fact, I'm much more likely to be hurt playing rugby, especially against boys at least two years older than me.'

The headmaster shook his head. 'I don't think so, and I really can't see how you could fit in two sports with your studies. You will have to give up this soccer.'

Eoin was shocked, but he wasn't going to back down. 'Well that's a shame, sir, because I was really looking forward to playing rugby and soccer together. But if you're telling me I can't play football then I will have to go back to my original plan and take a year off rugby.'

Mr McCaffrey's jaw dropped open. 'No, no, no,' he replied, 'you cannot do that.'

Eoin shrugged his shoulders. 'I just want to play with my friends, not boys two years ahead of me. I don't think that's being unreasonable, sir.'

The headmaster was used to getting his own way, but was now flustered, dismayed at how the conversation had turned.

'I-I-I'll have to talk to you about this later,' he said, before turning and walking away.

The boys returned to their table.

'What was that about?' asked Theo, one of their class-mates.

'That was just Eoin putting the headmaster in his place,' chuckled Dylan.

Eoin glared at his friend. 'That wasn't it at all,' he said.

'I just don't like being pushed around. I thought the head was being unfair and I told him so.'

Alan frowned. 'I hope he doesn't hold it against you – or the Red Rockets.'

CHAPTER 17

After breakfast, Eoin decided he wanted to be on his own and so changed into his trainers and went for a run around the school grounds. He trotted around the playing fields for twenty minutes before he took a breather, pushing through the bushes to his favourite hideaway, the Rock.

'Good morning, Eoin,' came a familiar voice.

'Hello, Brian,' Eoin replied. 'What has you around these parts today?'

'Oh, nothing in particular, I just seem to be zipping all over the place at the moment. What have you been up to?'

Eoin sighed, and explained about their excursion to Dalymount Park.

'And now the headmaster tells me I have to give up playing football. It's just not fair. I made it clear to him that if he did then I wouldn't be playing rugby either.'

Brian nodded, and told Eoin he had great sympathy for his position.

'But think about it,' he went on. 'Who does this hurt more – you or him? You will just end up doing nothing all year and miss out on a lot of great sport. You only have three years left in school, and you'll always regret this year if you just give up everything.'

Eoin shrugged his shoulders. 'I can't back out of it now. It would be letting down Alan and Dylan. And I know I am in the right on this one, he's the one being unreasonable.'

Brian nodded; he couldn't argue with Eoin on that.

'So what was the match like – I used to go to a lot of soccer games. I once saw Ireland play Italy at Lansdowne Road, a cracking match it was – I remember it as if it were yesterday. Although it was nearly a hundred years ago – 1927 I think.

'Ireland took the lead through our star player, Bob Fullam, but Italy won 2-1. Fullam had the hardest shot of any player I've ever seen – one free kick hit one of the Italians in the head and knocked him out cold. They were pleading with the referee not to allow Fullam take any free kicks after that!'

Eoin laughed. 'No there was nothing as dramatic as that. Dylan was all enthusiastic about seeing his beloved

Limerick, but he cooled a lot on them after they were beaten 5-1.

'When we were over in Dalymount Park we met an old man who told us all about the great players he had seen, he was a bit like a soccer version of you – only still alive,' joked Eoin.

'Very funny,' said Brian. 'I haven't met too many soccer ghosts down in Lansdowne Road – I think that Italy match was the last game played there for nearly fifty years.'

'So you would never have seen Liam Whelan,' asked Eoin. 'The old lad, Alfie, said he was the best player he ever saw. But he was killed in a plane crash when he was twenty-two.'

'The same age as I was when… when it happened,' said Brian.

'Wow, yes, of course. That's quite a coincidence,' said Eoin.

'No, I never saw him play, but his name is familiar. I hear all sorts of people being discussed,' Brian added.

Eoin decided it was time to get back to the dormitory and bade farewell to Brian. He had to sort out his uniform and clothes for the week ahead. 'At least I won't have to worry about sports gear,' he said to himself as he jogged back to the school.

CHAPTER 18

Eoin was relieved to see Dylan and Alan were not in the dormitory, so he lay down on his bed and stared at the ceiling to ponder his problem.

He knew Brian was right, of course, but Eoin didn't like to back down when he felt entirely in the right. He couldn't go a whole winter without playing something, he loved the camaraderie of the dressing room too much. But to bar him completely from playing football was unjust.

His head hurt from all the thinking so he closed his eyes and within a minute he had dozed off.

It was almost one o'clock when he awoke and realised he hadn't completed all the chores he had set himself to do that morning.

He hopped off the bed and quickly sorted out his clothes, filling a bag for the laundry, which he threw over his shoulder and headed down the stairs.

As he reached the bottom the front door opened and in walked Mr Finn, an elderly gentleman who had retired from teaching at Castlerock a few years before.

'Ah, Eoin, it's so good to see you again,' he said. 'And how are your family keeping?'

Eoin's father, and grandfather, had both been at school in Castlerock. Indeed his grandad, Dixie, had been in the same class as Andy Finn.

'They're all well, sir,' he replied.

'No need to call me "sir" any longer,' Mr Finn said, with a smile. 'But I do need to talk to you today. Will you meet me back here at quarter past two?'

Eoin nodded his agreement and went to drop his clothes to the laundry before heading for the dining hall in search of lunch.

There he met Dylan, Theo, Alan and Charlie, who were arguing about something as they polished off their apple tart and ice cream.

'Hey, Eoin, did you have a good nap? We called up to the room at one stage, but you were snoring your head off,' announced Dylan.

'Yeah, thanks for leaving me be,' Eoin replied. 'I had a bit of a headache.'

'That's not surprising,' said Alan, 'Are you alright mate?'

'You won't be alright when I tell you who's just been here,' said Dylan. 'Only the headmaster, and he told me that until the situation was resolved he would not permit soccer to be played on the school grounds.'

Eoin groaned, feeling his headache return.

'I'm still not sure what I'm going to do,' he told his friends. 'And I just met Andy Finn outside – he wants to have a chat with me after lunch.'

'Wow, Mr McCaffrey must have called him in to twist your arm,' suggested Dylan. 'Andy's sound though, he'll know what to do.'

Mr Finn was a gentle character, and had been a great help to Eoin when he was struggling to settle into Castlerock – not least through the excellent book on rugby coaching he had written many years before.

'Shall we go for a stroll around the fields?' he suggested to Eoin. 'It seems such a waste to be indoors on such a fine day.'

The pair rambled off, exchanging chit-chat about what they had been up to in the summer, and the new challenges Eoin was facing in Transition Year.

'Which, of course, brings me to your little dilemma,' said Mr Finn with a smile.

Eoin grinned weakly back at him. 'You've heard about it so?' he asked.

'Well, Mr McCaffrey rang me last night in quite a tizzy,' he replied. 'He tells me you are refusing to play rugby, which does seem a great pity.'

'It's not quite that simple, sir,' Eoin answered, before going on to explain about why he come to the decision he had.

Mr Finn let him speak without interruption until he had finished his story.

'Thank you for explaining that so well, Eoin,' he started. 'And I do think you have a point about the fairness of it all. Do you think you might see a way to returning to rugby if the headmaster gave his approval to the soccer club being set up and allowed use the facilities?'

Eoin chewed his lip. 'I would, but I don't think it's fair if he stops me from playing too. I don't want this to be all about me, but I really want to have a bit of fun playing light-hearted sport with my pals. I don't think it will get in the way of my rugby – and if it does then I'm happy to let soccer take a back seat.'

Mr Finn smiled. 'Well, I think we have room to manoeuvre there, Eoin. Let me take that to the headmaster and I will see if we can work out a compromise to suit all parties. You are such an excellent rugby player that it would be a shame to let that go to waste — but you are also an excellent friend to your pals and it would be terrible to interfere with that.'

CHAPTER 19

Funnily enough, Eoin and his pals were watching an English soccer match when the headmaster walked into the common room just after four o'clock.

'Ah, I thought you lot would be here,' he announced. 'Eoin Madden, can you step outside with me please.'

Eoin walked to the doorway to the sound of his pals' whispers – 'Good luck Eoin,' said Alan, and 'Give him a dig in the ribs if he says no,' from Dylan, miming a punch.

But there was no need for violence of any sort. Outside in the corridor was Mr Finn, who had a beaming smile on his face.

'Alright, Eoin, I've had a chat with Mr Finn and he explained a bit more about your position,' said the headmaster. 'I'm still not convinced you will have the time or energy to play both sports, but I am prepared to allow you to attempt it.

'A soccer club – I understand you wish to call your-selves the Red Rockets – will be permitted to be formed for TY students only and may use the school grounds for training and matches as long as they are not at the times allocated to rugby. But if you do play matches against other schools you must not use the name "Castlerock College".'

Mr Finn added: 'I think there are a set of portable soccer goalposts and nets that were used in the summer camp in the groundsman's shed. The headmaster has agreed you be allowed to use these too as long as you put them up yourselves and return them when you are finished with them each day.

'And I wish you best of luck with your efforts – I was an Arsenal supporter when I was younger and, if I'm not mistaken Mr McCaffrey here was quite a fan of Not-tingham Forest back in the day.'

The headmaster blushed as Eoin grinned and thanked both the men. 'We will not cause you any headaches, sir,' he told the head, 'and hopefully you will come along and watch us some time.'

Mr McCaffrey just nodded and walked away. Eoin thanked Mr Finn and promised to pass on his best wishes to Dixie and his dad.

He related the news to his friends who could hardly

believe their luck.

'And we have goals – and nets too?' said Dylan.

'I'll have a word with groundsman Billy about maybe marking out the pitch if we have any home games,' said Alan.

'Take your time with that sort of thing, Alan,' warned Eoin. 'McCaffrey's onside for the moment, but we wouldn't want to push him too far.'

So Eoin settled into his after-school routine of rugby twice a week on Wednesdays and Saturdays, gym on Tuesdays and Fridays, and football after school on Mondays and Thursdays.

'There's still plenty of time for other things,' he pointed out to Alan in the dorm one evening. 'Especially now we have much less homework and study time. I might take up badminton or something to fill in the evenings – and the Sundays,' he added with a grin.

Alan laughed, and went back to carefully clipping the list of Bohs fixtures from the newspaper and pinning them to the noticeboard in their dorm. He was interrupted by the sound of his phone ringing.

'Hello, Dad,' he answered, 'any news?'

Mr Handy chatted away about nothing in particular,

just asking Alan about his schoolwork and activities.

'Oh yes, Dad,' said Alan, 'that reminds me that I need to ask you something.'

He briefly explained about visiting Dalymount Park and meeting Alfie.

'And he said he knew Grandad, and had even played with him. He seemed a bit sad or something – did anything happen to Grandad?'

Mr Handy kept silent for a few seconds and then sighed.

'Well, that's very interesting, I'd love to meet that gentleman myself. The next time there's a home game perhaps I could collect you from school and we could go along – bring Eoin and Dylan too if you like. We could have a bite before the game too – I'll ring Mr McCaffrey to check it would be OK to take you all away for the evening.'

Alan thought that was a great idea and said he would get his pals to secure their own permission to go too.

He told his dad, 'I have all the fixtures on the wall here and Bohs are at home to Finn Harps on Friday week.'

'OK, well I'll get online and buy some tickets,' Mr Handy replied, 'and I'll text you the details of our outing.'

CHAPTER 20

The Red Rockets were starting to take shape as the better players began to emerge. Eoin hated to admit it, but Richie Duffy was probably the best outfield player they had – but Charlie was a seriously good goalkeeper.

They had enough players for two full teams and Dylan realised they would have to start playing matches against other teams to keep everyone interested. So he made contact with Ligouri College who they had played rugby against several times.

'They want us to play them on Monday after school,' Dylan announced after he checked his emails. 'We will have to go down to them first.'

'That's fair enough,' said Alan. 'We can get the Dart straight to the school. I'll check that it's OK with Mr McCaffrey.'

The headmaster gave his approval without comment,

and Dylan and Alan returned to the dorm to make a first draft of who they would have in the team.

'Charlie in goal,' started Dylan, 'then Andrew, Paddy, Ferdia and Theo across the back, Figo, Richie and Eoin in midfield, me and James out wide and Ernesto up front. Sam and Jin Chen on the bench, we'll sort the rest out later.'

'I can't argue with that,' said Alan, 'that Ernesto looks a serious goal scorer.

'He says he played Under 11s for Uruguay,' said Dylan. 'And their senior team won the World Cup way back.'

Alan laughed – 'yeah, they did – way, *way* back. In 1930 and 1950!'

'Are we all still wearing red?' asked Eoin, 'you'd better check everyone has a red shirt. I suppose the school rugby shirt would make more sense but McCaffrey probably wouldn't approve.'

'Ah we just have to wear red,' said Dylan, 'we'd look pretty stupid wearing green shirts if we're called the Red Rockets.'

'Yes, that's a fair point,' agreed Eoin.

By the day of the game they eventually amassed enough red shirts to cover the ten outfield players and three substitutes. If Charlie got injured he would have to give his yellow goalie shirt to his replacement, but fingers crossed that wouldn't happen.

'So we're basically a selection from Liverpool, Man United, Sligo Rovers, Bayern Munich and Munster,' said Theo as they lined up in their patchwork kit. 'I hope no one laughs at us.'

Down in Ligouri College, close to the Aviva Stadium, the hosts' coach welcomed them to the school, but was a bit surprised that they did not have a teacher with them.

'We're a sort of rebel soccer club,' explained Dylan. 'They're not very keen on us playing at all.'

The coach was amused, and impressed that they had set the team up themselves.

'We've some decent players,' he told Dylan and Alan. 'But I'll take them off at half-time to give a few others a run. It might make more of a game it for you. There's no point hammering you ten-nil now, is there?'

Dylan bridled at the suggestion his team could ever be beaten ten-nil, but decided – for once – not to say anything.

Instead he went back to his team and told them what the coach had said.

'We'll show him,' said Figo, whose real name was Johnny Murphy.

CHAPTER 21

The Rockets had a disastrous start, conceding a goal straight from the kick-off when Ligouri's big midfielder just ran at the centre of the defence – and they all just backed off. Charlie had no chance of saving the powerful shot and Dylan almost exploded with anger.

'That's appalling guys, you need to get your tackles in. That's why you're in defence, you need to close these fellows down and not let them get a shot at goal.'

Paddy and Ferdia looked a bit sheepish, but promised it wouldn't happen again.

But it did, and as the half-time whistle blew Ligouri led by three goals to nil.

'Don't be hard on the lads,' Eoin whispered to Dylan as they walked towards the rest of the team on the sideline. 'They're trying hard, they maybe just need a bit of organisation.'

Dylan nodded and called the team into a huddle.

'Look lads, they're obviously playing together for years – they look like a real team. But they have weaknesses and we have strengths, so let's work on making sure we see both of those in the second half.'

He went on to suggest a few changes in approach but didn't bring on any substitutes. His major change was asking Eoin to switch with Ferdia. Eoin agreed that it was a good move.

'I like it back here,' he confessed to Paddy. 'You can see more of the game and see danger developing. I hope Ferdia doesn't mind swapping places.'

'I doubt it,' Sam replied. 'He loves scoring goals and he has a much better chance up there.'

The game resumed with Ligouri having taken off all their better players which gave the Rockets a little bit of confidence. Richie – who had been very quiet in the first half – had a bit more time on the ball and was starting to find his range with passes into the feet of Ernesto. The South American striker was very fast and his first shot thumped against the post with the goalkeeper beaten.

That seemed to pep up the Rockets even more and they dominated the next ten minutes. And all their pressure paid off when Dylan hared down the left wing and fired in a low cross which Ernesto stretched to reach with his boot. But he got there, and the striker steered the ball wide of the keeper and into the net.

The Castlerock boys were delighted and were even more so when they won a corner with fifteen minutes left. Eoin came up to join the attack at the near post and flicked the ball back with his head. It reached Dylan at the back post who swivelled and struck the ball power-fully into the roof of the net.

'Three-two!' roared Alan from the sideline, where he was patrolling with a clipboard and pen. 'We can do this Rockets,' he added.

The Ligouri coach – who was refereeing the game – looked very worried, especially as he knew he couldn't bring his best players back on.

Dylan tried to keep his players going, bringing on Jin Chen for Theo for the last ten minutes. But try as they might, they just couldn't score. With one minute left Ernesto burst through for a one-on-one with the goal-keeper who came out towards the striker. Ernesto went to flick the ball wide of him with the outside of his boot but the keeper grabbed his foot and he stumbled, and the ball trickled harmlessly wide.

The ref blew for a goal kick, refusing to answer the Red Rockets' appeal for a penalty. From then on he was very keen for the game to end and blew up after barely a minute of injury time. Dylan was furious for a few seconds, but Eoin suggested he forget it as it was only a friendly. Dylan nodded and went over to shake the ref's hand.

'Thanks very much for the game,' Dylan told him. 'We really enjoyed it and gave you a bit of a fright there.'

'You certainly did,' said the coach, 'we won't be messing about with substitutes when we play you up in Castlerock.'

Dylan grinned back. 'And there won't be any talk of ten-nil next time either,' he said.

The coach smiled. 'Well I learnt my lesson there,' he replied. 'You've some excellent players and once you play together a few times you'll be a test for lots of teams. The Football Association runs a special competition for schools that usually just play rugby. There are about seven or eight teams in it – you should ask can you enter. You definitely won't be the worst team in it.'

CHAPTER 22

As soon as they got back to school Dylan went online to investigate the FAI competition and sure enough it had seven entries, so he emailed them right away to suggest Castlerock could make up the numbers to an even eight.

He got a positive reply next morning and was told that if he paid the seventy euro entrance fee by five o'clock that day they would be in the first round draw.

Over breakfast, the friends discussed what would happen next. 'We've a problem here lads,' Alan said. 'McCaffrey doesn't want us to play as Castlerock, but the FAI rules say we have to play under the school's name.'

'It would be best if I talk to him,' suggested Eoin, 'I'll tell him the other schools that are playing and he might not feel so hostile.'

Eoin caught the headmaster in a good mood, and

once he explained who they would be taking on, and for a maximum of three games, he relented.

'But I still want total priority for the senior cup team, Eoin,' he threw in as he left.

Eoin and Alan spent the morning break collecting five euro a head off the soccer squad and getting the school secretary to transfer it into the FAI bank account. They were in the cup!

The week flew by with the combination of lessons, activities and training sessions, so Friday afternoon was a welcome break from it all for Eoin. His dad, and Dylan's mam, had sent emails to Mr McCaffrey confirming they could leave the school grounds for an excursion with Mr Handy, and the boys changed out of their school uniforms with growing excitement.

'This Finn Harps crowd are pretty good,' said Alan. 'I was reading the newspaper reports since I knew we were going to see them. They're second in the league and have a really good young striker that all the English scouts are watching.'

'It should be a good game so,' said Eoin, draping his new red and black Bohemians scarf around his neck.

'I think I'll support Bohs too,' announced Dylan,

'just for tonight though, I'm not deserting my beloved Limerick Football Club just because they lost.'

'Lost 5-1,' Alan reminded him.

Dylan scowled, but Eoin hurried them both out the door before any real trouble started.

They waited at the front of the school, fielding a bit of banter from the senior boys about their soccer scarves, until Mr Handy arrived.

'Hop in boys, we have a bit of time before kick-off so we'll go get you a pizza, or whatever you prefer.'

'That would be lovely, Mr Handy,' replied Dylan as they all crammed inside the car.

They found a restaurant about ten minutes' walk from the ground and quickly ordered their food. While they were waiting Mr Handy asked Eoin and Dylan did they know about his family's connection with Bohs.

'Alan was asking me about his grandfather – who used to play for Bohemians – and why he stopped playing,' he began.

'It is still a bit of a mystery to me. I know he was a very good player, but was injured, came back and then just gave up. He never talked much about football – I confess I didn't have much interest in it when I was growing up – and I never got the chance to ask him.

He's gone now, so I never will,' he said, sighing.

'I'm hoping this Alfie character will be able to fill in a few gaps – especially as he saw him play.'

CHAPTER 23

The boys demolished their pizzas and started the stroll back up towards the ground. Alan's dad bought them all a drink and a bar and bought himself a Bohs scarf. He offered to buy Dylan one too, but he put up his hand like a Garda on traffic duty, saying: 'I won't be going there Mr Handy, thanks. It's glorious Shannon blue or nothing for me.'

The boys laughed and walked on, soaking up the atmosphere as they joined hundreds more streaming towards the stadium.

At the ground Alan suggested they watch from the same place as last time. 'You show Dad where we're sitting Dylan – me and Eoin will have a look for Alfie.'

It didn't take long as the stand was still less than half full and Alfie cut a familiar figure with his white beard and ancient black and red bobble hat. They explained that Phil Handy's son was waiting to meet him at the back of the grandstand and he told them to lead the way.

Mr Handy stood when Alfie arrived. 'I'm very pleased to meet you,' he said, offering his handshake.

'And you are Phil's son,' Alfie replied with a smile. 'You're a ringer for him.'

They all sat along the back row, and Alan's dad explained that he knew very little about his father's football career. Alfie told them about how he was a star schoolboy player with Home Farm and had every club in Dublin knocking on his door looking to sign him up when he was eligible.

'But Phil was a huge Manchester United fan, and he knew all about a young local lad who had left Home Farm for Old Trafford only a couple of years before. He idolised Liam Whelan – almost everyone did around here – and one day he came home from school to see a big black taxi standing outside his house.

'Out came Liam, the manager Matt Busby, and the famous United talent scout Billy Behan. They all went inside – word spread quickly and soon everyone in Phibsborough and Cabra was hanging around in the street waiting for them to come out. They signed autographs for about an hour when they did and off they went for the plane back to Manchester.'

Alan's dad smiled. 'I never heard that story, I'm sorry

to say.'

Alfie nodded. 'I suppose he was heartbroken the way things turned out,' he replied. 'The story was that your father was to go over to Old Trafford that summer, once he was finished in school, and would sign for them as an apprentice player.

'Well, everyone was very excited for Phil, but once the word got out that he was on his way to a big career he became a bit of a marked man. Football was brutal in those days – every team had a clogger, a hit-man whose job was to try to take out the opposition's best players. Phil got plenty of attention from cloggers, but he was well able to dance his way out of any trouble.

'But one day, about two weeks before he was due to get the boat over, he came up against a shower from… I won't say, they're probably a lot nicer crowd these days. But back then they had a bad reputation and they went after Phil. He was kicked from one side of the field to the other, but just before the final whistle he got a vicious kick that broke his ankle.

'He was never the same after that. I remember him telling me how his mother had to go to a neighbour's house to ring Manchester and ask to speak to Matt Busby, and how she had to explain that Phil wouldn't be coming over for a while.

'He never did go over. It took him months to get back to fitness and he was never the same player again. He was still good though – he signed for Bohs then and we got a couple of excellent seasons out of him. Liam Whelan kept in touch, he used to write to him and called up any time he was home in Cabra – he lived over in St Attracta's Road there,' he pointed off to his left.

'Phil had one really good run when he scored a clatter of goals and when Liam came to watch him one Sunday afternoon he rattled in a hat-trick against Drumcondra. Liam asked him would he be interested in going across again and Phil said he'd get back to him.'

Alfie blew his nose and took a deep breath before resuming his story.

'But whatever decision he made, he never got a chance to tell Liam. A week or two later, well, the Munich crash happened and that was that. Poor Phil was devastated – he was so upset that he retired from football at the end of that season, and him not even twenty-one years of age.'

Mr Handy rubbed his eyes and thanked Alfie. 'That explains so much,' he told him. 'He hadn't even met my mother by then and she never knew the whole story. I'm sorry now I never asked him about it.'

'Ah, he probably wouldn't have talked about it,' the old man replied. 'He idolised Liam and I suppose he wondered, if things had played out different, whether he might have been on that plane too. But one thing is for sure – they were two great footballers, and their clubs and country missed them something terrible.'

CHAPTER 24

The old man stood up. 'Well thanks for listening to me nattering on there. It's great to see you lads back here – you certainly brought our boys a bit of luck last time, and we'll need it again tonight.' And off Alfie went for his pre-match cup of tea.

'Wow,' said Alan, 'that was some story, wasn't it?'

'Yes indeed,' said his dad. 'We'll have to do a bit more research into this. I'd love to read some of the reports of the games he played.'

'The biggest mystery of all, of course,' Dylan said, 'is how a brilliant player like him could have a grandson who is *brutal* at football.'

Even Alan joined in the laughter.

'I don't know,' he responded. 'Now it's proved I've got some talent in my bloodline, maybe I ought to test it out at training on Monday.'

They settled back to enjoy the game, which finished

in an entertaining 1-1 draw, with their new hero Seb Joyce firing in a sweetly-struck volley just after half-time. After Mr Handy had brought them back to school the trio went to the common room to tell their pals how their excursion had gone. The room was quiet, just a handful of boys watching television, playing chess or games on their phones.

Charlie leapt out of his chair to greet them.

'Hey, Eoin, have you seen the senior team for tomorrow?' he asked. 'They've a friendly against St Kevin's – and you're in the match-day 23.'

Eoin's face fell. 'Really? That's the first I've heard of any match. I've had only a handful of training sessions with them. It must be a mistake.'

But it wasn't a mistake, as Charlie pointed to the noticeboard where the rugby team was posted.

Eoin hardly slept that night, tormented by the idea that he would have to come on as a replacement for the school's top team and not a little fearful of taking on much bigger and stronger players.

'These guys are all in the gym every day,' he protested to his friends the following morning. 'The only dumb-bell I know is Dylan... Sorry Dyl!'

'It's a home game at least,' said Alan.

'But that only means there'll be loads of guys watching,' said Eoin. 'They normally wouldn't go to watch a friendly, but once they hear I'm playing half of Transition Year will come along.'

CHAPTER 25

And of course Eoin was right. Even his team-mates were surprised at how many spectators had turned out for an early-season friendly on a Saturday morning.

'They must have heard we had one of the British and Irish Lions playing for us,' suggested Ross Finnegan with a broad grin.

Eoin smiled thinly. He felt uncomfortable anyway, but he really hated being the centre of attention.

'Madden, I don't expect you will have to play too much,' said Mr Carey, 'but I'll bring you on for the last ten minutes to give you a taste of the big boys.'

Eoin didn't feel reassured by this – and was even less so when he saw the St Kevin's College boys.

'They… they're fully grown men,' he said to himself as he ran out for the warm-up.

Eoin had seen plenty of big, tough boys in his three

years on Castlerock's junior cup team, and his games with Leinster, Ireland and the Lion Cubs. But they were all lads his own age, give or take a year or two. The opposition today had *stubble*, even full beards.

Happily Castlerock's out-half, Milo McGeady, came through the first half unscathed and with his team leading by nineteen points to nil Eoin hoped Mr Carey would forget about giving him a game.

He also knew he would never be so lucky, and sure enough with about ten minutes to go Mr Carey whistled to the remainder of the unused subs to start warming up. Eoin ran up and down the touchline, receiving a mixture of mild abuse and encouragement from his classmates.

'No bother to you, Eoin,' roared Dylan as he passed him in the crowd.

Eoin smiled, but inside he was feeling quite uncomfortable. At the next break in play the referee ushered on the replacements and Eoin took his place at out-half.

For the first couple of minutes he escaped having to do much more than pass the ball on to the inside centre. But with Castlerock on the attack, they won a line-out just outside the opposition 22 and the scrum-half, Odran, fed the ball back to him. Time was tight – he could feel the St Kevin's tacklers bearing down on him

– but he took a neat sidestep and chipped a lovely ball over the defence and watched as it tumbled into touch a couple of metres from the try-line.

'Great kick, Eoin,' came the roars from his team-mates, as the visitors had just realised who had arrived in their midst.

'That's that Lions fella,' grunted one.

Ross Finnegan won the ball in the lineout and the forwards formed a maul around him, pushing and heaving till they collapsed over the line and the referee signalled the try.

'Great work, Eoin, you set that up for us brilliantly,' said Ross as they trotted back. Eoin realised he would be taking the conversion, but he hurried his kick and it sliced wide.

The game resumed and Castlerock were still well on top as the final whistle neared. From a scrum around half-way, the number nine fed the ball back to Eoin who again kicked for touch. But as his kicking foot touched the ground again – long after the ball was gone – Eoin was floored by the St Kevin's open-side flanker.

Eoin hadn't seen him coming, and was stunned as he hit the ground with force. The referee blew up and awarded a penalty – 'That was far too late,' he told the St Kevin's player, adding, 'if there was any more time left

I'd give you a yellow.'

Once the initial shock of the tackle wore off, the serious pain from his ankle wore on, and Eoin roared in agony. He was afraid to look at his foot and noticed that the referee's face had gone white.

'Medic, please,' shouted the ref, ushering on the trainer who had first-aid training. Mr McDermott took one look at the injury and took out his mobile phone.

'You'll be OK, Eoin,' he said, 'the ambulance will be here in five minutes.'

He told Eoin not to look at his foot, but he had already worked that out for himself and had no intention of doing so. He tried to concentrate on willing the pain away and thinking of happier times.

CHAPTER 26

It was only after Eoin had treatment in the hospital emergency department that the pain started to lessen, and he actually dozed off for a few minutes. When he woke up he realised that must have been the medicine and he asked the doctor how bad was the injury.

'Well, we've had a quick look and we'll be sending you for an x-ray shortly. I won't speculate about it – but I suspect you won't be playing rugby for a few months anyway.'

Eoin slumped in his seat – disappointed not so much about missing rugby, but about not getting to play with the Red Rockets.

When he came back from being x-rayed his friends were waiting for him.

'That was a shocker of a tackle,' said Dylan, 'a few of the sixth years had a word with your man in the dressing room afterwards. He won't be coming back to Castlerock in a hurry anyway.'

Eoin smiled and asked had either of them got a phone he could borrow. Alan opened the entry for Eoin's dad and handed over his mobile.

'Cheers, Al, but I always ring my mam first with bad news. Dad would fly off the handle and drive straight up here; Mam knows how to explain it to him sensibly.'

Sure enough, Eoin's mother was shocked and upset, but she quickly regained her composure and started asking about the important-for-mums stuff like whether he would miss any lessons and did he have clean pyjamas if he had to stay over in hospital.

'I'll be fine, Mam,' he finished, 'the lads are here with me and Mr Carey sent a message that he would collect me when I'm ready. Text me later on my own phone, I'll pick it up soon – and give my best to Dad and Dixie.'

Eoin handed back the phone to Alan, who asked the question that had been bugging him and Dylan since the incident.

'Well Eoin, do you think you'll be OK for the soccer thing, the Gillespie Cup?'

Eoin sighed, and told him he didn't think so, but as he was explaining why the doctor returned.

'We have the x-rays back,' he told Eoin, 'and it's not as bad as I feared.'

The doctor opened a large brown folder and showed him the image of his damaged ankle. 'You see here — well if it *was* broken you'd see a bright white line, but there hasn't been any break. It's been badly sprained though and you will need a bit of ice for the next while, then you will be on crutches and plenty of rest for a few weeks.'

'So when can I play sport again?' he asked.

'We can have you up and running around in three or four weeks,' he said, 'but rugby or football? Don't even *try* it for six weeks.'

Eoin's face fell, and his pals' joined it in sympathy.

'But I can give you exercises to do,' the doctor added, 'and if you do them every day I could see you back playing quickly enough.'

Eoin thanked him and the doctor left.

'That's a disaster,' said Dylan. 'Our first match is in just three weeks, you've no chance of playing in that.'

'You'll be fine without me,' Eoin replied. 'There's plenty of better footballers than me, I was only making up the numbers.'

'No way,' said Alan, 'You were a big part of our plan to sort out the defence,' he said.

'We'll have to look at a few more of Alan's twenty-three plans now,' Dylan said with a grin.

CHAPTER 27

Mr Carey brought Eoin and the other boys home that evening, but he hardly said a word to them in the car journey back to school.

'Thanks, sir,' Eoin said as he hobbled up the steps with the aid of his new crutches.

'No problem, Eoin, and I'm sorry your first Senior game ended the way it did.'

'Oh well,' he replied, 'I probably shouldn't have been up against guys that much bigger than me anyway.'

Mr Carey gulped and nodded. 'Well, good luck with the rehab and if you need any help getting around give me a shout.'

When they got back to the dorm – Eoin had been granted the rare privilege of a key to the staff lift – Dylan started to laugh.

'Well you certainly told him what you think of forcing you to play against older lads. He might think twice next time,' he said with a chuckle.

'Yeah, I just wanted to make that point,' Eoin replied. 'I'm sure he'll make me pay for it down the line, but I enjoyed letting him know he was in the wrong.'

Alan went to lie down on his bed when he noticed someone had left a small parcel under his pillow.

'Your father called in while you were out,' read the attached note, which was signed by Mr McCaffrey.

Alan tore open the packet, and was perplexed to discover it just contained a card and a pair of very old black and red football socks.

The note on the card read: 'These were your grandfather's Bohs socks. They might bring you a bit of luck. Dad.'

'Well that decides it,' Alan announced. 'I was thinking of giving football a proper go. Now there's a vacancy on the team – *and* I have a legend's socks. What could go wrong?'

And sure enough, on Monday afternoon Alan joined the Red Rockets for training. He and Dylan had spent an hour the previous evening having a kick-about on the back field, allowing Alan to get used to some of the basic skills he had neglected since he played on a team in primary school. He also rediscovered how fearless he was in tackling opponents.

'I'm too small to play central defence,' he told Dylan, 'but I can read a game well and know when I need to get forward, so I could definitely do a decent job as a full-back, preferably on the right.'

Dylan nodded. 'Andrew's not the best, but you're going to have to win his place off him. Let's see how you go in training – I'd be reluctant to make a big change in the defence at this late stage, especially seeing how ropey it was in the friendly.'

Alan agreed, and promised he would work hard to earn his place.

He was first to arrive for the Red Rockets' training session and checked the goalposts were in place and arranged the cones for the warm-up drills.

'Fair play, Alan,' said Dylan when he arrived. 'Good to see your new enthusiasm now you're a player-coach.'

When the rest of the Rockets were ready Dylan filled them in on Eoin's injury and gave them the news that the return friendly against Ligouri would be the following Friday. 'So I want to see a good turn-out for the extra session at 5 o'clock on Wednesday,' he told them.

Alan wasn't very fit so he found the pace of the

training hard to get used to, but by the time the inter-squad ten-a-side finished off the session he was feeling better. He was even able to keep pace with the opposing winger as he raced down the wing, and closed him down so he was unable to get in a cross.

'Good work, Alan,' said Dylan as they collected the cones after the game. 'I won't be too worried if Andrew gets injured. I'll have you in the match-day fifteen for the friendly anyway.'

Alan grinned, and felt ten feet tall walking back to the dorm where Eoin was lying on his bed with his foot in the air.

'How was that?' he asked Alan.

'Great!' came the reply. 'We're starting to look more like a team anyway. Which reminds me...'

Alan rummaged in his schoolbag and took out his art copy.

'What do you think of this?' he asked, showing Eoin a red and white logo of a rocket with flames emerging from the back of it. The name of the team was curved around the bottom of the circle.

'That's class, Al,' Eoin told him. 'But who is this team that calls themselves the Red Rookets?'

Alan snatched the copybook from him and realised with horror that he had misspelt the name of the team.

'Just as well you spotted that, I was going to get it printed up for our team-sheets.'

CHAPTER 28

Eoin's ankle returned to normal dimensions after a day or two and lots of ice, but he wasn't able to get around on it very much – classroom, dining hall and bedroom were pretty much the limits of his horizon, with a couple of short steps outside for some fresh air.

'Will you be able to get around to watch the Ligouri match?' asked Alan when they were sitting on a bench outside the main entrance to the school. 'It will be on the back pitch. Billy was asking about the proper dimensions and how to line the field. I think he was a bit worried about the big centre circle – up to now he's only done straight lines for rugby.'

'Tell him to get a piece of string and a peg,' Eoin suggested. 'Put the peg in the middle of the half-way line and he could make the line-maker into a giant compass like we use in maths. As long as he keeps the string stretched it will be fine. Same with the 'D' on the penalty area, only he doesn't do a full circle.'

'That's amazing,' said Alan. 'Did you come up with that yourself?'

'No,' Eoin replied. 'When I was down in the Aviva a couple of years ago Brian made me watch the ground staff when they were converting it into a soccer pitch.'

'Wow,' Alan replied. 'That's a great idea. Can you sit here on your own for a minute while I go down and tell him?'

Eoin sat back on the bench and closed his eyes. It was rare to get a moment of peace in a boarding school, and he enjoyed those times when he did. But it never lasted long.

'Eoin, are you asleep?' came the call. Eoin opened his eyes to see Brian standing in front of him.

'I haven't got very long,' Brian explained, 'but I just wanted to check if you had seen anything happening out of the ordinary. We're getting a lot of disturbance in the atmosphere and a lot of murmurings that there may be trouble ahead.'

Eoin pointed at his foot. 'Only this, I suppose,' as he explained about his damaged ankle. 'And, yes, we went back to Dalymount and the old guy told us about Alan's grandfather, who was a really good footballer. He knew that fellow Liam Whelan who we talked about before.'

'OK, well if you think of anything else, I'll drop down to the Rock every evening around seven o'clock, if you can't make it that far' – he nodded towards Eoin's foot – 'send Alan along instead.'

And with that he disappeared, just as Alan rounded the side of the building.

'Billy's delighted,' he reported, 'I think he's going to go around in circles for the whole morning with his new toy.'

'I hope he doesn't get dizzy,' laughed Eoin, before he told him about his visit from Brian.

'Yeah, and I'll keep an eye on the Rock till you're out and about,' Alan agreed.

CHAPTER 29

The Ligouri College team arrived just as Alan and Dylan had finished putting in the corner flags. Their coach jogged over to talk to them.

'The pitch looks fantastic,' he said. 'Your groundsman looks like he knows how to prepare a soccer pitch too.'

Alan grinned. 'Yeah, I'll pass that on, he'll be chuffed.'

They agreed that the Ligouri coach would referee, as Alan couldn't get any of the Castlerock staff to admit they knew the laws of football. Alan himself was one of the named substitutes and was huddled with the others when Eoin hobbled around the corner of the building just as the game kicked off.

Eoin noticed what his friend was wearing.

'I love your socks, Al,' he called, pointing to the woolly black and red footwear. 'They're impossible to keep up,' Alan replied. 'I'll have to get some elastic for the next game.'

Eoin noticed that there was quite a few of the boys from the younger classes watching, and some even started chanting, 'Castle-rock, Castle-rock.'

'I hope Mr McCaffrey doesn't hear that,' he told Alan, with a smirk.

The chanting seemed to inspire the Red Rockets as they started to look more like a team than in the first game, although they were punished for a mix-up at the back and Ligouri had a one-nil lead at half-time.

'We're going well,' said Dylan, 'Just keep it tight in defence and we'll surely create a couple of good chances for Ernesto as the game goes on.'

Dylan took Alan aside to say he would make a couple of changes fifteen minutes into the second half and to keep the subs doing their warm-up exercises.

Unfortunately, Dylan had to change his plan when Ligouri extended their lead just after the break and Theo took a knock shortly afterwards.

'On you come, Alan,' shouted Dylan as Theo limped off. 'Ronan, can you warm up too?' he added. 'I'll have you on in five minutes.'

Alan took Theo's place at left back, which wasn't ideal as he was really only able to kick and tackle with his right foot. But he was always willing to get stuck in with a task, so Eoin had no worries that he wouldn't acquit himself well.

'Pull your socks up, Alan,' Eoin said as Alan next ran past him.

When he next had a chance, Alan stooped and pulled the socks up as high as he could, but they were far too big for him and they slid down his calves almost immediately.

A loose ball ran towards Alan, and he surprised himself at how smartly he was able to trap it and set off on a run upfield.

'Give it here, Alan,' shouted Richie, but the substitute saw a gap had opened up and he moved wider down the line. As he reached the left edge of the penalty area he paused before curling a cross into the box. The ball sailed over the heads of the Ligouri central defenders and fell to Ernesto, who picked his spot and powered a header into the net.

The Castlerock crowd erupted, and the players mobbed their South American star. It was only as they ran back to half-way that his team-mates realised that it had been Alan who delivered that perfect cross. They ran to congratulate him too.

'And that was with your left foot!' laughed Dylan. 'That was amazing Al, brilliant ball.'

'Right, now let's get the equaliser,' Alan told them.

'We have them rattled now.'

Ligouri were certainly rattled, but they were a strong, experienced team and they allowed very little room for the Castlerock midfield to operate. The Ligouri striker hit the post with Charlie beaten, but the margin was still only one goal when the game entered the last five minutes.

The word had spread about Ernesto's goal and the Castlerock support had doubled – even a few teachers were now looking on, although a couple watched from the windows on the first floor of the senior block.

'This is amazing,' said Dylan during a break in play, looking at the huge crowd that had gathered. 'Let's give them something to be proud of.'

Richie won the ball in midfield and beat his man. Racing in on goal he saw Ernesto was marked by two defenders so he let fly himself. The ball cannoned off the crossbar to a huge roar of disappointment from the crowd. But they didn't suffer too long – the ball fell to Alan on the corner of the penalty area. He trapped the ball, took one look at the goal and curled the ball wide and over the keeper's head into the top corner of the net.

Poor Alan was swamped by his team-mates, and could hardly walk when he finally emerged from under the pile-on. Happily enough he didn't have long to worry about that as the referee soon sounded the final whistle on a sporting 2-2 draw.

CHAPTER 30

For the rest of the evening, Alan and Ernesto were mobbed – indeed all the Red Rockets got plenty of pats on the back in the dining hall and around the school. The younger kids all wanted to know when the next game was – and could they join the club.

Dylan had to explain that the football club was for Transition Year boys only, but he suggested they ask Mr McCaffrey.

After dinner, Alan – still in his football kit – ran down to the Rock to check had Brian any messages for Eoin. He was stunned to see he had two other men with him, one in the black and red stripes of Bohs, the other in the famous red shirt with white collar of Manchester United.

'Hi Alan, sorry to give you a fright there,' said Brian. 'But I came across these lads and they really wanted to come and visit you. You might recognise one of them too.'

Alan looked at the men's faces again, and sure enough he saw something in the face of the Bohs player. The ghost was a lot younger than the photographs in his hallway at home, but his features were unmistakeable.

'Grandad?' he asked.

'I am indeed,' replied Phil. 'Delighted to meet you – Alan, isn't it? – you'll have to tell me all about your father and how he's getting on.'

Alan smiled – 'I think I can guess who your friend is here, too,' he said. 'You're Liam Whelan, aren't you?'

'Yes, that's right,' he replied with a grin. 'I see you're wearing a Liverpool shirt – you don't support them do you?'

'No!' Alan replied, 'I actually support Leeds United, but we have a school football team and I had to wear a red shirt – I borrowed this off my mate Charlie.'

Alan sat back against the Rock and turned to Phil.

'We only found out all about your football career recently,' he told him, explaining about his visit to Daly-mount and meeting Alfie.

'Ah, is Alfie still around?' he asked, 'He's a lovely lad, but he must be a fair age by now. A great Bohs supporter and not a bad little player in his day.'

'We brought Dad to meet him last week, he was delighted to chat to him about you and your football.'

Phil smiled. 'That's nice. I never talked to him much about it and he was more interested in cars and books when he was young so I didn't push it with him. At least there's one footballer still in the family.'

Alan blushed. 'Nah, I'm not that good…' before he paused, and added, 'well I suppose I'm not bad – I just scored a cracking goal to force a draw.' The football legends appeared to be impressed as they listened to him describe his score.

'Well, I hope you keep up the football,' said Phil. 'This seems like more of a rugby school, Brian was telling me.'

Alan looked at Brian, before turning back to the footballers. 'So why exactly did you want to come here?' he asked.

Liam shrugged his shoulders. 'We're not sure, lad. We keep hearing about trouble brewing around our old stomping ground, as well as some talk of history repeating itself. Brian here got involved and told us about your pal Eoin and how you have a habit of solving mysteries like this.'

'He's right about that,' said Alan. 'Eoin has a knack of meeting the ghosts of famous sportsmen – we've met Dave Gallaher, Michael Hogan and William Webb Ellis and a few more. He'll be delighted to add you to his collection. But they all seem to bring trouble with them…

'But how did you know to come here?' he asked the football ghosts.

Phil pointed down. 'It sounds stupid, but it just came to me in a dream – a message to "follow the stockings". I recognised them immediately.'

Alan laughed. 'Dad dug them out of the attic, I think I'm going to have to get mum to sew some new elastic in.'

'And get your dad to buy you a *proper* red shirt,' suggested Liam.

'I will,' Alan laughed, as he prepared to leave.

'By the way,' Phil asked. 'We must come and watch you play some time. What did you say your team were called?'

'Well, that's a funny story,' Alan answered, 'before we ever heard of you we decided to call them the Red Rockets.'

The two footballers stared wide-eyed at the boy.

'The Red Rockets,' Liam repeated. 'There's a name from the past. Well, it looks like we've come to the right place, Phil.'

CHAPTER 31

A few days later in the common room, Dylan opened his emails to find another message from the FAI, telling him that the Red Rockets had been drawn away to St Osgur's in the Gillespie Cup quarter-final.

'Your old buddies,' he told Eoin. 'I'd say they'll be delighted when they see you on crutches.' Eoin had played several matches against St Osgur's on the rugby field, and usually came out on top.

'Yeah, but I should be off the crutches by then,' said Eoin. 'I'm going to try to get back playing as soon as I can.'

'That would be great, but there are no guarantees about your place. We've a lot of competition now, and it's going to be impossible to drop Alan after his worldie against Ligouri.'

'No worries,' Eoin replied, 'I'm happy to fight my

way back into the team. I doubt if I'll be ready for a while yet though.'

Alan joined the pair and suggested they pick the team for the first cup game, arguing that it would be good to play the eleven together against the next-best players in training that evening.

'Just so they can work out where everyone else is,' he said.

'Right so, but let's do it down the Rock,' suggested Dylan, 'that United legend might be back on a visit.'

Eoin hoped so too – he had been a little bit jealous that Alan was the one who was there to meet the footballers, although of course as one of them was his friend's grandfather he was probably more entitled to be.

There was no sign of the ghosts at the Rock, but while the boys were discussing the make-up of the team, Brian appeared on his own.

'Hey, Brian,' said Eoin, 'no sign of the star players tonight?'

'I'm afraid not,' Brian replied, 'everything has quietened down on that front. I'm not sure where the lads even are this week.'

'Maybe you need to wear your Bohs socks for them to appear,' Eoin suggested to Alan.

'I hope you're wearing shin guards under those socks,' Brian said. 'The last thing Castlerock needs is another injury like Eoin's,' he added, nodding at the patient.

'We might have another excursion to Dalymount once Eoin gets off the crutches,' Alan suggested. 'Would you able to come along, Brian? It would be great to see Liam and Phil again.'

Brian said he would see what he could do but again urged the boys to be careful.

Within a week Eoin was free of the strapping and crutches, and the pain had pretty much gone too. He was able to walk, but the school nurse advised him to hold off running for a day or two until he built up a little more strength.

He volunteered to act as linesman for the cup game against St Osgur's, who were indeed delighted to see he wasn't going to torment them on the pitch. The game was played in a public park far from the school, so there were no Castlerock supporters present. Mr McCaffrey had allowed them to travel in the school minibus, and he asked Mr Finn to go along to ensure the boys came to no harm.

The Gillespie Cup was designed to give schools that

normally didn't play soccer a chance to try out the game. Although St Osgur's had been in the competition before, they weren't very good and Castlerock were soon on top and had a two-nil lead at half-time.

'That's great stuff lads,' said Mr Finn, who joined them in the huddle during the break. 'But you need to put more pressure on their left back, he's very unsure of himself.'

Dylan looked a bit puzzled. 'I didn't know you knew anything about soccer, sir?' he said.

'Well, I wouldn't pretend to be more than a mere student of the game, but I've been supporting the Gunners for more than sixty years. They even used to win leagues and cups along the way.'

Most of the boys jokingly booed his choice of club, except Ferdia who was wearing his own Arsenal shirt.

'I suppose you're not used to seeing you team winning two-nil at half time?' asked Alan, as the Gunners were famous for winning many games by a single goal.

'I expect you to double the score in the second half,' said Mr Finn. 'And if any of you have forgotten my Maths classes from first year, that means four-nil.'

CHAPTER 32

Mr Finn didn't get his way, but he was even more delighted as Red Rockets trooped off after beating St Osgur's five-nil, with Ernesto completing his hat-trick and Richie scoring the other two.

'That was very impressive,' Mr Finn told the boys on the bus back. 'And while Ernesto and Richard certainly took the plaudits, I was most pleased today with the performance of Charles Bermingham between the posts. I always think a goalminder is the most important position on the team and once you have a good one you can build a team from there.'

Charlie blushed, but Eoin was happy that his role had been highlighted – it was a team game and too often the goal-scorers hogged all the credit.

'Who have we got in the next round?' asked Cillian.

'The Osgur's coach told me we would be playing Springdale Secondary,' Dylan replied.

'Did we ever play them in rugby?' asked Alan.

'I don't think so,' replied Eoin, 'that Andrew Jacks went there – he was the lad who missed out on the Wolfhounds trip to London after Marcus McCord crocked him.'

'I wonder will we be at home this time?' Dylan wondered, and asked Mr Finn if he might ensure they were allowed to host a game if they got a home draw.

'I can't see why not,' he replied. 'Hasn't Billy done a great job on the pitch – and once the game is out of school hours there will be no disruption.'

And sure enough, next morning Dylan got confirmation that the semi-final would be staged on a ground of the Red Rockets' choosing.

'You'd better go and work your charms on Mr McCaffrey,' Alan suggested to Eoin. 'Tell him your ankle's nearly better and you're mad keen to get out there kicking the oval ball.'

Eoin grinned. His foot felt a lot better today and he resolved to get some light jogging to see how it had improved. He knocked on the headmaster's door and was told to enter.

'Hello, Mr McCaffrey,' he started. 'Can I have a word

with you about football?'

Sitting at his desk, Mr McCaffrey peered over his glasses and lowered the sheaf of papers he was reading.

'Football? I don't know much about football, I'm glad to say,' he replied.

'Oh, it's not that bad, sir,' Eoin replied. 'We had our first cup match yesterday – and we beat St Osgur's five-nil.'

'Five-nil? So just the one try in the game? That seems very low-scoring,' he said.

'No sir, it was football – and five-nil is quite a hammering.'

'Oh, very good,' replied the head. 'Congratulations.'

'Thank you,' said Eoin, 'and that's why I am here. We're in the semi-final now and we've been drawn at home. I was just checking that it would be OK to play the game here, on the back pitch.'

Mr McCaffrey frowned. 'Hmmm, I'll have to ensure we don't need it for rugby. It's very disruptive having football games here, so if you do play this here then it will be the last home game. We can't have parents and past pupils thinking we're no longer a rugby school.'

Eoin nodded, not keen to get into any deeper argument.

'Thank you sir, I'll check with Billy if there is any

rugby booked in for that date. Even if we win, the final won't be here so it will be the last game anyway.'

Mr McCaffrey was still muttering to himself as Eoin left, and went straight to confirm the fixture with Billy.

'That date is fine, Eoin,' the groundsman told him. 'I'll have the pitch looking like a snooker table by the time of the semi.'

Chapter 33

'I see Bohs are at home again on Friday,' Dylan read. 'It's an FAI Cup match.'

'I know,' Alan replied. 'But dad is away on business and he really wanted to come. We'll have to get special permission to go.'

'I'd say we'll struggle with McCaffrey,' sighed Eoin. 'He's got a real downer on football, I think he's terrified everyone's going to give up rugby just because of the Red Rockets.'

'That's mad,' said Dylan. 'No one will ever shift rugby in this school. Why can't he just let us have a bit of fun?'

'I'll see if I can catch him at the right moment – again,' Eoin promised, before they headed off for another yoga session.

By the following evening Eoin still hadn't asked Mr

McCaffrey. He steeled himself for the inevitable resistance and decided to catch him after dinner. He kept an eye on him in the dining hall, and as soon as the head stood up, Eoin made a beeline for him.

'Excuse me, sir,' he started. 'There's a match on Friday that Alan, Dylan and I would like to go to.'

Mr McCaffrey frowned. Eoin steeled himself for the rejection, but Mr Finn, who had been dining alongside the headmaster, smiled.

'Is this Bohemians again?' he asked. 'I would love to go along if you chaps wouldn't mind.'

The principal shrugged. 'Well, if you don't mind ensuring they all get back here in one piece, Andy, that's fine by me,' he said.

'Excellent,' said Mr Finn. 'I'll meet you at the front of the school at half past four on Friday so, Eoin. Do I have to wear a scarf and wave a rattle?'

'If it gets cold I'll lend you my scarf,' replied Eoin, 'but there's no need for the rattle, whatever that is.'

Mr Finn explained how football fans used to wave a noisy wooden rattle when he was young, and from the sounds of it, it wasn't missed in modern stadiums.

'No, I think we'll teach you a few of the chants and you'll be fine then, thank you, sir – and thank you headmaster.'

Alan and Dylan were delighted that the way had been cleared for another football excursion, but they were concerned that Mr Finn might cramp their style.

'We won't be able to talk to Liam and Phil if Mr Finn is there,' complained Alan as they walked back to their room.

'I know,' said Eoin. 'We may have to run a diversion – Alan might be the best one to talk to the ghosts.'

'I suppose it's *his* grandad,' Dylan agreed.

Friday came around quickly, and the boys were looking forward to having Mr Finn along. Since he retired as a teacher he was a lot more relaxed and he became a bit of a funny man, always cracking corny jokes with the boys.

He turned up at the school wearing a quite ridiculous red and white woollen cap with a huge cannon in the middle, the famous symbol of Arsenal football club.

'This is my lucky charm,' he explained to the boys. 'If I wiggle my ears the gun goes off.'

'It's probably a good idea to leave it in your pocket, sir,' Eoin suggested. 'It's a warm evening and there's no sign of rain. You'll be the only one in the ground wearing a hat – especially one for a team not playing.'

Mr Finn laughed and pocketed the cap. 'It's been far too long since I went to an association football match.

You will have to guide me though the correct behaviour this evening. I trust you won't lead me astray.'

CHAPTER 34

The boys managed to get in early enough to secure their usual seats at the back of the stand. Bohs were playing Ballsbridge Rangers in one of the many Dublin derby matches and the ground filled up quicker than usual.

'This is quite exciting,' said Mr Finn as he watched the crowds sway and chant even before the game had kicked off.

'Are you a Bohs fan, sir?' asked Dylan.

'Well it's very late in life for me to making a new commitment, but I do like their shirts and their name reminds me of a very enjoyable holiday I spent in Czechoslovakia – as it was called then – many years ago.'

Dylan looked puzzled.

'That's where they get their name from I think,' explained Mr Finn. 'The west of the Czech Republic was once made up of an old kingdom called Bohemia.'

'I suppose that's as good a reason as any to support a team,' said Eoin. 'I'm not even sure why I've become a fan — I think it was just to go along with Alan.'

'Well, that's quite a good reason too,' said the old teacher. 'It's nice to go along to matches with your pals. This could become a life-long pursuit for you.'

They joined in with the crowd singing the Bohs favourits 'Hold me Now' before they settled back to watch the game, and again Bohs' striker Seb Joyce was the star of the show.

'He's very fast on his feet, isn't he,' said Mr Finn. 'I was reading about him in the newspaper this morning. It seems there will be some scouts here from some of the big English clubs. They say he could be worth millions.'

'You'd hate to lose him, wouldn't you?' said Alan, 'But Bohs could do an awful lot with that sort of money. They could keep the club going for years and buy some really good players too.'

Joyce rattled the woodwork twice before he finally scored a brilliant individual goal that brought almost the entire stand to its feet. Eoin noticed that even those wearing Ballsbridge Rangers colours were applauding.

'That was a splendid shot,' announced Mr Finn, waving his red and white cap above his head.

The boys looked at each other, mildly embarrassed by

their companion.

Half-time arrived and Alan winked at Eoin.

'I'm going to get a drink, would you like a cup of tea, Mr Finn?' he asked.

'That's very kind of you, thank you,' he replied.

'Will you come too Eoin, to help me carry them?' asked Alan.

The pair scampered down the gangway and ducked in under the stand. But instead of heading for the tea-stall they found the hallway outside the bar and stood looking at the photo of Liam Whelan and the famous Busby Babes team.

'Are you lads looking for me?' came a voice from behind them. Liam had appeared, wearing his United kit, and alongside him stood Phil.

'Yeah, we were hoping we'd bump into you,' said Alan.

'It's funny, you're the second people to look at the photo in the last few minutes,' said Phil. 'There was a couple of men here who studied the picture closely – they've just gone into the bar.'

'They were English lads, Manchester by the sound of their accents,' Liam told them. 'They pointed me out in the picture and said Joyce could be the next big signing from Dublin.'

'He's a darling player, isn't he?' said Phil.

'They were talking about bringing United over to play a friendly as part of the deal, that would be a real money spinner for Bohs,' added Liam.

'Wow, I'd love to see that,' said Alan.

'Have you heard any rumblings about any trouble?' asked Eoin. 'It's been quiet back in school, although we're in the semi of the cup on Monday. You should come out to Castlerock to check us out.'

The boys said their goodbyes and dashed off to get Mr Finn his tea and themselves some soft drinks. By the time they got back to their seat the game had restarted and Ballsbridge Rangers had equalised.

'That was unfortunate,' said Mr Finn, 'your absence probably cost your team that goal.'

'Ah, don't hang that on us, sir,' said Alan. 'There was a big queue.'

CHAPTER 35

Bohs rallied and Joyce scored a second goal with a shot from fifteen metres out.

'How does he hit it so hard,' wondered Dylan, as they saluted the score.

'He just seems to have so much time,' noted Mr Finn. 'He gets himself in position to shoot and can pick his spot. He's a very special player.'

'He ees indeed,' said a man sitting in front, who turned around and grinned at them. 'I haf came all ze way from Paris to watch him, he ees a magical talent.'

Unfortunately Bohs couldn't hold on to the lead and with seconds left to play Ballsbridge forced the ball into the net from a scrappy corner.

'Is it penalties?' asked Dylan as the referee blew the final whistle.

'No, it goes to a replay,' answered Alan. 'We have to play them in the RDS in two weeks.'

'Well, that was very exciting,' said Mr Finn, 'I'll have to see about getting tickets for the replay so.'

As they walked slowly towards the exits, Dylan spotted two men chatting beside the entrance to the tunnel.

'That's Kenny Butcher, he's United's assistant manager,' he told his pals. 'He played on the team that won the Champions League ten years ago.'

'They must be the pair that Liam and Phil saw downstairs,' Eoin whispered to him.

'I'd love to get his autograph – is that OK, sir?' Alan asked the retired teacher.

Mr Finn nodded and the boys walked over and politely asked the former star would he mind signing their match programme.

'No problem lads, are you Bohs fans?' he asked.

'Yeah, and I support United too,' Dylan added quickly.

'What do you think of that lad Seb Joyce?' Kenny asked.

'He's amazing,' they all replied together. 'Best player we have,' added Alan.

Kenny nodded in agreement as he finished signing.

'Are you going to buy him for United?' asked Eoin.

Kenny laughed and introduced the man beside him as their head scout. 'Well I do hope so, we think he would be a great player at Old Trafford too.'

A tall gentleman wearing a long black coat stepped forward. 'Mr Butcher, I'm Gerry Flanagan, I own the Ballsbridge Rangers. Bohs are very lucky indeed to have a talent like Joyce.'

The pair shook hands, and he introduced him to the United chief scout.

Eoin tugged Alan's sleeve, signalling to him that they should hang around for a minute or two.

'And how much do you expect to pay for him?' asked Flanagan.

'A player like that we would normally offer eight to ten million pounds,' he replied. 'But did you see the grandstand there? There's scouts from Chelsea, City, Spurs, and a couple from France and Spain too. This guy is one of the hottest prospects in Europe right now. I suspect he could fetch up to twenty million.'

The Ballsbridge owner whistled. 'Wow, that's about twenty-five million euro – that would be a game changer over here. Bohs could buy up all the best players and coaches – and win everything for the next ten seasons.'

'Aye,' said Kenny Butcher, 'If you ever get a lad half as good as him make sure and give us first dibs on him please.'

The men all went their separate ways and Eoin and

Alan rejoined Dylan and Mr Finn.

'That was very interesting,' Alan said, before relating the conversation between the three adults.

'I can see what he means,' said Mr Finn, 'A sum like that would means Bohs would dominate football here for years to come.'

CHAPTER 36

Billy had the field looking immaculate for the Red Rockets semi-final, which was more than could could be said for their collection of jerseys.

'Three Man U, two Arsenal, two Liverpool, one Sligo Rovers, one Bayern Munich and one Munster rugby shirt, plus Charlie in Liverpool green,' sighed Alan. 'I wonder if we sold Ernesto to Bohs would we get enough to buy a nice red kit that made us look like *a team*?'

'At least you have a proper pair of socks this time,' said Dylan.

Alan looked at his feet. With a rising feeling of panic he realised that he wasn't wearing his grandfather's socks.

'Oh no,' he cried. 'I left them in to be washed and they haven't come back yet.'

Eoin, who had agreed to act as linesman again, teased his pal: 'You'll be rubbish without them,' he told him.

Alan looked worried, but with only seconds to kick-off he couldn't do much about it.

A crowd twice as big as that which attended the previous friendly had come out to watch and they cheered the referee as he blew the whistle to start the game. Red Rockets kicked off and quickly got on top of their opponents, St Malachy's. Their pressure paid off in the eighteenth minute when Richie Duffy broke through the defence and slotted the ball into the bottom corner of the net.

Alan wasn't enjoying the game however, and the missing socks were preying on his mind. He had started at right-back and his opposing forward had a bit more pace than Alan. Twice in the middle of the half he was beaten on the outside and allowed get a cross in, which sent Dylan into a rage.

'Come on, Alan, get your tackle in,' he roared after the second mistake.

'Sorry Dyl,' Alan mumbled, relieved that Jin Chen had headed the ball away safely.

But Alan continued to struggle, and just before half-time a loose ball fell to him on the edge of the Rockets' penalty area. He swung his leg to clear it upfield but miskicked and the ball squirted off his boot into the path of the St Malachy's striker. He recovered from his surprise to fire a low drive past Charlie to make the score one apiece when the whistle blew for the interval.

'Ah, Alan, that was just brutal,' said Dylan when they gathered in a huddle. 'You're having a nightmare there. We'll leave you on for the next while but if you don't settle we'll bring on Theo for the last half hour.'

Alan nodded, and excused himself from the group, dashing across to where Eoin was standing chatting on the touchline.

'Hey, Eoin, can you do me a big favour – can you check is our laundry back in the room? And if it's there can you bring me those old Bohs socks? I'm playing so badly and I'm sure it's the socks…'

Eoin agreed and trotted off to the dormitory, delighted to get a chance to test his recovering ankle.

Sure enough, the socks were in their room and he upped his speed on the return journey. Alan spotted him coming and immediately kicked off his boots.

Pulling on the black and red socks, he thanked Eoin, who wished him luck.

'Hurry up there, full-back,' called the referee, 'we're all ready to start.'

Alan tied his boots quickly and signalled to the ref, who restarted the game. With the ancient socks on his feet, Alan felt a foot taller, and everything inside him seemed to race quicker too. He was much more confident in his play and his first chance with the ball at his feet he hoisted a pass over the midfielders to the feet of Figo Murphy who skipped past the full back and rocketed the ball to the net.

'Wow, that was some pass,' Dylan told him. 'You're like a new player.'

Red Rockets held their lead, and the only blip came with ten minutes to go when Ernesto was floored in the area and the referee pointed to the spot.

'I'll take it,' said Richie, taking the ball from the Uruguayan.

It was a poor penalty however, and the ball was comfortably saved by the St Malachy's goalie.

The huge crowd erupted at full-time, and they chanted the name of the school as well as 'Er-nes-to, Er-nes-to' for a long time afterwards.

CHAPTER 37

As he went into the dining hall that night, Eoin smiled as he heard the first years still chanting the star forward's name on the other side of the room. Richie Duffy came in behind him and Eoin extended his hand towards him.

'Well played, Richie, that was a cracking first goal,' he told him as they shook hands.

'Thanks Eoin, I'm enjoying the soccer, sorry you got crocked there, will you be back soon?'

Eoin filled him in before they went off to join their own pals.

At the seniors table he was seated with Alan, Dylan and Charlie.

'Thanks again for going on the hunt for the socks,' Alan told him. 'They certainly made me play a lot better.'

Eoin smiled. 'I'm not sure about that Al, you've worked hard to turn yourself into a class player now. Those socks won't last forever, so you need to start believing in yourself without them.'

'What did you think about Richie snatching the penalty away from Ernesto?' asked Dylan.

'Well, on one level I respect his confidence that he wanted to take it,' Eoin replied. 'But it's the job of the coach and the captain to decide on the penalty taker. If you weren't happy you should have stepped in.'

Dylan nodded. 'Well he won't be taking the next one. We'll have a competition at practice tomorrow to see who is best at taking penos and they can have the job.'

'We might all need to practise them,' said Charlie. 'If the final ends in a draw it goes to penalties.'

'Speaking of the final, any idea when it will be?' asked Eoin. 'I'm definitely up to some light training, and you never know I might be right for the final.'

'If selected!' replied Dylan. 'We've a sound team who've got us into the final, so we'll be careful about making changes.'

'Fair enough,' said Eoin. 'I'm not sure I could play a full game anyway – but I might be able to do a job for you off the bench.'

Next day, after checking his email, Dylan rushed to join

the boys at training. 'You won't believe who we've got in the final,' he started, 'only Ligouri College!'

'Brilliant, we could beat them!' said Charlie.

'We *did* beat them,' Alan reminded them.

'Are we at home this time?' asked Theo, 'or down in their place?'

'No,' grinned Dylan, 'we're going to have to get a bigger bus for this one – it's going to be held in Dalymount Park.'

'That's amazing,' said Eoin. 'At least we'll know how to get there.'

The squad were buzzing for the session and the time passed quickly. Figo, as usual, won the keepy-uppy competition before Dylan called them together. He explained that the final would be decided on penalties in the event of a draw, so they needed to practise them, and they needed to decide which five players would take part if it was needed.

'So, any volunteers for penos?' asked Dylan.

Richie, Ernesto and Figo all put up their hands immediately, as did Dylan. A few of the guys who hadn't played yet, like Benjy and John, also volunteered.

'James? Andrew?' asked the skipper. The boys shook their head.

'Alan?'

'OK,' he agreed. 'But we'll need more than five if it goes to "sudden death". Everyone should at least practice them in case they are needed.'

Each player had two shots at Charlie in goal, but only three of them scored twice – Duffy, Ernesto and Alan.

Eoin had joined in the practice part of the session, but once they started a squad match he went off to do a few laps of the field. The penalty competition was nearly over when he rejoined the group.

'Can I have a go?' he asked, and Dylan nodded.

Eoin put the ball on the spot, took a short run, and planted it in the bottom left corner of Charlie's goal. He put his second kick in the top right corner.

'That's pretty good,' said Dylan, 'you're in the semi-finals now.'

Only Ernesto and Eoin scored with their next shots, setting up a 'final' showdown to decide who would take spot kicks in a match situation.

Eoin was about to take his first kick when he stopped. 'But I'm not likely to be playing at Dalymount,' he said. 'There's no need for a final of this – Ernesto is the man for the job.'

He shook the striker's hand. 'Just make sure you get plenty of practice in,' he joked. 'Ligouri have some tough tacklers and we might be lucky enough to get a penalty this time with the neutral referee.'

'We'll train on Saturday morning instead of Friday this week,' Dylan told them. 'We're going to watch a big cup match in the RDS – I might even pick up a few ideas.'

CHAPTER 38

Ernesto spent a lot of time over the next few days perfecting his penalty technique with Charlie, who was delighted to get the practice at saving them.

'I hope you get a chance to use these skills now,' laughed Eoin as he helped them tidy up after practice. 'And try not to think about everyone watching you from the stands.'

Ernesto stopped and glared at him. 'Thanks for nothing, Eoin,' he replied. 'I hadn't thought of that before you brought it up.'

As they were packing away the cones, Mr Finn walked across the field towards them.

'Good evening, boys,' he called. 'And congratulations on your victory – I will certainly be there at the final. But I have a small problem tomorrow.'

'Oh no, will you miss the Bohs replay?' Eoin asked.

'No, not at all,' the retired teacher replied. 'But I will

be unable to travel into Ballsbridge with you. I have an appointment nearby and can meet you, say, an hour before kick-off – you are well able to get the bus there on your own, I presume.'

'That's fine,' replied Eoin. 'Will we meet you outside the library?'

'Perfect,' said Mr Finn. 'I'll see you there at six o'clock.'

There were more congratulations for Eoin and his pals after dinner that night, when Mr McCaffrey called down to their table.

'I'm pleased that you have done so well in this competition,' he told them. 'And I have received several phone calls from past pupils passing on their well wishes. I was worried they might object to the College playing association football, but all the calls have been very positive.

'I will ask the games master to organise a coach for the boys who want to go and support you, and of course the mini-bus will be at your disposal for the team,' he told them before pausing. 'I may even be in attendance myself,' he said with a smile.

Once he had left the boys stared at each other in

astonishment.

'Well he's changed his tune, hasn't he?' said Alan, with a wide grin.

Eoin invited Charlie along to the Bohs game on Friday evening, so the four pals got the bus together just outside the school. They arrived in Ballsbridge almost two hours before kick-off, so they decided to hang around the public park to kill time.

'We should have brought a ball,' moaned Dylan, 'I'd love a kick-about.'

'And then they'd have confiscated it on the way into the ground,' pointed out Eoin.

As they sat on a bench in Herbert Park deciding what to do, Liam Whelan suddenly appeared in front of them. The Busby Babe looked worried.

'Lads,' he said, 'we got a message this morning saying there was trouble brewing back in Dublin. We were sent here – Phil is off having a scout around too. Keep your eyes peeled,' he said, before disappearing again.

The boys were a bit rattled by Liam's brief visit and set off towards the exit. They came across a small pavilion selling tea and sandwiches, and as they were feeling thirsty bought some soft drinks and sat down at the tables outside. Alan gave Eoin a dig in the ribs.

'Don't look now,' he started, 'but that guy who said he owned Ballsbridge Rangers is sitting behind you. He's talking to two men who look like footballers – they're wearing Ballsbridge training jackets.'

Eoin nodded and slumped back in his seat, signalling to his pals to keep silent as he attempted to listen in on the conversation going on behind him.

The tall man, Gerry Flanagan, was doing most of the talking.

'…and it's important to make it look like an accident,' Eoin heard him say. 'We don't want to have any blame come back to us at all.'

'Right,' said one of the men. 'But *why* do you want us to do it?'

Flanagan sighed. 'Because if Bohs get twenty-five million for Joyce they'll have so much money to spend on players – and improving their ground – that they will dominate our league for years to come. United say they will come and play them in a friendly every year too, which will bring in hundreds of thousands more.'

'OK,' said the other man. 'And what's in it for us?'

The tall man reached into his inside pocket and took four envelopes out, which he split into two small piles. 'As a down payment, there are five hundred euro in each of these two envelopes,' he said, patting the first pile. 'If you do your job and the transfer is cancelled, this will be for you,' he added, pointing at the other two envelopes. 'There's five thousand each in them.'

The footballers nodded. 'So we have to go in hard and break something – I suppose an ankle or shin would be the best?'

Flanagan agreed, and checked his watch.

'We better head over to the RDS now. And I can't stress enough that this must remain between us and no one else. If a word of it gets out I'll deny any knowledge – and you will be looking for a new club.'

CHAPTER 39

The trio left, leaving Eoin to recount their conversation to his stunned pals.

'That's shocking behaviour,' said Charlie. 'We have to try to report him.'

'Who to, though?' wondered Alan. 'A Garda would just laugh at us if we told him what we heard.'

'How about Alfie,' suggested Eoin. 'If we could find him he might know who to talk to.'

'Good idea,' said Dylan. 'I'd say he'll be in with the main group of Bohs fans. Let's head over and see if we can spot him on the way in.'

As they walked through the park towards the ground, Eoin thought about what they would say to Mr Finn. He would surely find the plot hard to believe, and maybe try to persuade them to keep out of it for fear of bringing trouble – or worse – on themselves.

They walked past a man reading a newspaper – the

back page headline read 'Joyce transfer latest – Barcelona will bid.'

Eoin thought of the young man whose whole life would be transformed by such a move, or *any* big move – not to mention his family and his football club. He also thought of Phil Handy and how an injury ended his chances of a professional career just as he was on the brink of fame and fortune. He had to act – and act fast.

'Alan, can you keep Mr Finn occupied for a few minutes, I'm going to see if I can find someone.'

Eoin took off at speed towards the back entrance of the park, raced up some narrow streets before arriving at a busy main road. He crossed at the traffic lights and climbed the steps into a grey stone building.

'Can I speak to Detective Sweeney please?' he asked the garda at the desk, who frowned and picked up the phone. 'What's it in connection with?' he asked Eoin.

'An assault,' he replied.

'When did this happen?' asked the garda, still waiting for the phone to be answered.

'It hasn't happened yet,' replied Eoin.

The garda's face darkened – 'Are you wasting my…' he started, but luckily for Eoin a voice came on the line.

'…Oh hello, Detective Sweeney, there's a young fella at the desk here wants to talk to you about an assault.'

Eoin waited on a bench until the officer arrived.

'Hello there, Eoin,' she said with a smile. 'What adventures are you up to now?'

Eoin had first met Detective Sweeney when he foiled the theft of the Rugby World Cup trophy a couple of years before. She had led the garda unit that retrieved the cup with Eoin's help.

He explained what he had heard, pleading with her to prevent the evil plot.

She asked him to wait in the reception area while she went to make a couple of calls and returned five minutes later with another garda.

'Right, hop in,' she told Eoin as a squad car pulled up outside. 'We'll need you to show us who's who at the stadium.'

They sped off, siren blaring, towards the ground. 'I love that noise,' the detective told him. 'It makes me feel like I'm in a TV cop show.'

Eoin grinned back and watched as other cars slowed to let them pass, and the crowd of supporters parted as they neared the stadium.

'We'll go in the back gate,' said the driver, 'I've radioed ahead.'

The car pulled up alongside the old grandstand at the arena, which was built to watch show-jumping and had been converted into Leinster Rugby's home ground.

As Detective Sweeney made a phone call, Eoin spotted his pals with Mr Finn – and they were talking to Alfie.

'Excuse me, can I get out please,' he asked the driver.

'Hang on a minute, son, I'll have to check with the detective,' he replied.

Eoin tried to wave through the window as his pals neared the car, but they couldn't see him.

'Are you alright, Eoin,' asked Detective Sweeney when she finished her call. 'Who is that you're waving at?'

'My pals, and a Bohs supporter,' he replied, as they disappeared from view into the back of the grandstand.

'Well you'll catch up with them shortly,' she said. 'I've been instructed to hold off any action until the serious crime squad get back to me – they have had their eye on Gerry Flanagan for a while. We've been told not to approach the club until the half-time interval.'

'Half-time?' gasped Eoin. 'But it could be too late by then! We need to tell Seb and the manager.'

CHAPTER 40

Detective Sweeney shrugged. 'I'm afraid they are my orders.' She requested Eoin to go over the whole conversation in Herbert Park once again, asking him questions about the men and what they looked like.

She checked her watch. 'This match is starting in five minutes. Do you want to join your friends and meet me back here in half an hour?'

Eoin nodded and checked his ticket, pointing out to her where he would be seated in case they needed him earlier.

As he walked to his seat the players were out on the pitch warming up – but he couldn't see any sign of Seb Joyce.

'Eoin, Eoin,' called out Alan, waving at him as he neared where his friends were sitting.

Eoin found his way along the row and joined them.

'I saw you talking to Alfie,' he said. 'I was in the

Garda car.'

He explained what had happened since he last saw them. 'But they can't do anything until half-time,' he added with a frustrated sigh.

'Well then,' replied Mr Finn, 'it's just as well that the boys found that Alfie chap.'

'Yeah,' said Alan with a wide grin. 'We told him about the plot and he said he'd talk to the Bohs manager. Alfie was able to talk his way in and suggest they keep Seb on the bench to buy a bit of time. The Bohs boss was a bit nervous about missing his star player, but he was so horrified by the plan that he knew it was the best thing to do.'

Eoin relaxed. 'That was a great idea,' he said. 'I just hope they don't need him.'

As the teams lined up, Eoin spotted the two Balls-bridge players who had met Flanagan in the Park tea-rooms. He noticed that one of them was looking from player to player around the Bohs team, obviously con-fused by the absence of Joyce.

When the stadium announcer called out the teams, there was more confusion among the spectators, espe-cially when the star player was named as one of the substitutes. Eoin noticed the two Rangers players had looked at each other and shrugged their shoulders. He felt angry at their casual reaction, that they could treat a plan to hurt another player so lightly.

The stadium was packed when the referee blew the whistle for the game to commence.

Perhaps Bohemians were rattled by their late change of personnel, but they seemed to find it hard to settle. Ballsbridge, in contrast, seemed to get a bit more pep from the knowledge that the Bohs star man was absent.

The result was that Rangers were soon dominating the game and only some stout defending stopped them taking an early lead. But that was all undone by a slip in midfield which gave a Ballsbridge attacker an opening. He charged through, saw the goalkeeper coming out to him, and deftly chipped it over his head. The crowd held their breath as the ball bounced slowly across the goal-mouth ... and trickled over the line to give the home side the lead.

'Come on Bohs,' roared Alan, 'you can do it.'

But there was no doubt they were missing Seb Joyce and they rarely looked like equalising.

'Bring on Seb!' roared a spectator sitting nearby. 'We're useless without him!'

That led to a few mutters of agreement among the fans, but Charlie told Dylan that he wished they would be more patient.

Eoin looked at the stadium clock and stood up. 'I have to go guys,' he told them. 'Hopefully, I'll be able to do my bit for the Gypsies too.'

Down behind the grandstand Detective Sweeney was waiting with a group of fifteen uniformed Gardaí.

'Ah, Eoin, great to see you – I was just about to send someone to get you,' she said. 'We've got the approval to detain the three men you saw in the park, so I'll need you to follow us inside.'

She explained the plan to Eoin and the rest of the force. They left four men outside guarding the exit and made their way towards the dressing rooms.

Eoin checked the clock on his mobile – it was two minutes before half-time.

The group split up, with four officers walking up the stairway towards the directors' box. The rest made for the home dressing room.

Detective Sweeney told the steward stationed outside to open the locked door and once inside they waited at the back of the room. The detective asked Eoin to wait in the showers.

A minute or so later Eoin heard the whistle blow for half-time and the Ballsbridge Rangers' supporters cheer their side off the field.

Within seconds he heard the distinctive sound of football studs clicking across the cement floor as the teams made their way down the corridor.

oin peered out from the door of the shower area as the dressing room door opened.

'You should have taken that corner...' started a Ballsbridge player before he stopped dead, realising there were half a dozen Gardaí in the room.

'What's this?' asked the Rangers captain staring round the room. 'And who's the kid in the Bohs scarf?'

Detective Sweeney stepped forward. 'Please, we need all the players in here now,' she told them. Eoin spotted one of the men who was in on the deal was starting to inch backwards towards the doorway so he tugged the sleeve of one of the Gardaí and pointed out what was happening.

'You!' the Garda called out. 'Stay where you are,' as he moved across and took the man by the arm.

Sweeney looked at Eoin who nodded at the player, whose name was Lally.

'Right,' she announced, once all the players were in the dressing room and the doors closed.

'I apologise for detaining you like this, but it will be only for a few minutes,' she explained. 'We have become aware of a plot involving three members of Ballsbridge Rangers to stymie a transfer involving your opponents and an unnamed foreign club. We need to investigate this as a matter of urgency – which is why we are here at this moment.'

The door opened and two policemen led in Gerry Flanagan, who was loudly complaining.

'How dare you interfere with our club during an important fixture,' he shouted at the detective. 'I'll have you know that the Minister for Justice is an old school friend of mine...'

The detective held up a sheet of paper. 'This is a search warrant, which permits me to search this room and the persons of you and two of your players. Guards, please remove everything from the pockets of Mr Flanagan – and from the kitbags of these two players...' She waited while Eoin pointed out the other plotter, Molamphy the full back.

The rest of the Ballsbridge players were stunned, but no one spoke in support of them.

Flanagan erupted once more, but two guards held his

arms while Detective Sweeney searched his pockets. It didn't take her long to find two thick brown envelopes.

'That's the gate takings for today,' Flanagan whined. 'One of the security staff gave them to me just after kick-off.'

'We have had you watched by plain-clothes gardaí for more than an hour before that, and no one handed you anything,' she countered. 'But don't worry, we will check these for fingerprints,' she added, before moving on to the two players.

'Mr Lally and Mr Molamphy,' she began. 'We have been made aware that you have accepted a sum of money in return for breaking the leg of one of the opposition players today, namely Sebastian Joyce.'

The policemen opened each of the men's kitbags and rummaged around inside. They found Lally's envelope tucked inside his shoe and Molamphy's hidden inside a water bottle.

'It looks like you have something to hide there gentlemen. But we will have to discuss it further down at the Garda Station in Donnybrook. Please accompany me, we have nice separate cars for each of you.'

As the Detective left, she stopped in the doorway and turned back. 'And by the way,' she started. 'Apologies for the interruption. And the very best of luck to you in the rest of your match.'

The referee arrived just as she was leaving, telling the teams it was time to get back out on the field.

The shocked Ballsbridge players trudged back out with their manager desperately trying to reorganise the team formation and selecting which two substitutes to bring on to fill the gaps.

'Thank you, Eoin,' said the Detective when they met up outside. 'I'll need you to come back up to the station shortly to give us a full statement – and get your friends to come along too.'

She paused as a roar went up in the stadium behind her. 'But for now, young man, you need to get back upstairs and cheer on your team.'

CHAPTER 42

Eoin rejoined his pals just as Bohs won a corner at the Anglesea Road end. He quickly filled them in on what happened downstairs.

'So they're now missing their two toughest defenders,' chuckled Alan as the ball sailed into the goalmouth.

'Yeah, they look like they're in a bit of a mess,' Eoin replied.

The Rangers keeper punched the ball clear and the ball was hacked upfield.

Eoin spotted Detective Sweeney had returned to the arena and was making her way on to the touchline. She approached the Bohemians bench and said something to the manager, shook his hand, and left once again.

'I bet you we'll see Seb warming up very soon,' he told his pals.

And sure enough, within seconds the young Bohs striker was taking off his tracksuit and getting ready to take the field.

When the stadium announcer called out his name, the black-and-red-wearing members of the crowd erupted in delight. Joyce ran on to the field and took up his position at the front of the attack.

'Go on, Seb, let's see what you can do,' shouted Alan, much to the embarrassment of his companions.

Maybe it was Alan's shout of encouragement, or maybe it was the forty-five minutes he had spent kicking his heels, but Joyce was playing with even more energy and commitment.

And when the ball next came to him in space, two metres outside the penalty area, he looked up briefly to check the goalkeeper's position and curled the ball over and around him and into the net.

The roar could have been heard on the other side of the city as Joyce stood and waited for his team-mates to swamp him.

'That was a fine goal,' nodded Mr Finn. 'I once saw a lad called Liam Whelan score a goal like that when I was very, very young.'

His three young companions stared at him: 'Really? *You* saw Liam Whelan play?' asked Alan.

Mr Finn nodded and urged them to watch the play as Bohemians were on the attack once more.

Bohs tiny winger was racing down the wing in front of where the boys were seated. As he reached the corner he swung his boot and lifted the ball into the penalty area. The cross was met by the Rangers tall central defender, but he only succeeded in heading it out to Bohs midfielder Samuel Kealy Farren who let fly with a fierce volley, which went in off the post.

The four boys jumped out of their seats and hugged each other – at least until Dylan remembered that he was still a Limerick supporter.

'This is a rout,' said Mr Finn. 'Ballsbridge almost seem to have given up.'

'I think they're just a bit shocked about what happened down below,' said Eoin.

'And so they should be,' said Alan. 'I'd say the league might even relegate them for this.'

Seb scored another and Bohs eventually ran out winners by four goals to one, securing them a place in the final against their biggest rivals Shamrock Rovers.

'We'll have to see about getting tickets for that,' said Mr Finn. 'They usually have it in Lansdowne Road but since Eoin wrecked that ground they'll have to find somewhere else. Maybe Bohs will give you some free tickets after you saved their star player.'

CHAPTER 43

The newspaper front pages were full of the story of the foiled plot, but Eoin was happy that no one reported on his role in the affair.

'I got enough attention over the Aviva collapse,' he told Alan next day as they went for a run around the grounds. 'The last thing I need is Flanagan's mates calling around to make me change my story.'

'I think you've been watching too many television cop shows,' laughed Alan.

They arrived at the Rock and took a breather.

'Come on, Brian, show yourself,' joked Eoin, disappointed not to see his friend at his usual spot.

'Give me a minute, you're very impatient,' came a voice from behind the bushes.

Eoin grinned when Brian came into the glade.

'I was only joking, Brian,' he told him. 'But it is good to see you.'

The boys told Brian about their exciting day in Balls-bridge, which the ghost listened to with ever-widening eyes.

'This must be what Liam and his friend were talking about,' Brian replied. 'They'll be delighted to hear that you were able to help.'

The trio chatted for several minutes more before Eoin checked the time.

'We had better go Brian, we've got to get to training – it's the last one before the Gillespie Cup final.'

The training session went well, but Dylan seemed in a distracted mood when they sat down to eat in the dining hall afterwards.

'What's bugging you, Dyl,' asked Charlie. 'Pre-match nerves?'

'Yeah, a bit like that,' sighed Dylan.

'What's the problem,' asked Eoin, 'anything we can help with?'

Dylan frowned. 'I don't think so, unless you know how to defy the laws of mathematics.'

Alan looked at him with a puzzled expression.

'The problem is the team for the final,' replied Dylan.

'I thought it picked itself,' said Charlie.

'I wish you were right,' said Dylan. 'The last game we finished up with Charlie in goal, a back four of Alan, Paddy, Cillian and Theo, the midfield is Figo, Richie and Ferdia, with Dylan, James and Ernesto in attack. But with Eoin coming back I have a bit of a headache now because you can't get twelve into eleven slots.'

'What's the problem?' asked Eoin. 'I haven't played at all in this competition. It would be really unfair to drop Cillian, he hasn't missed a training session and he's played really well. I'm fit to play, but I'm not going to take someone else's place who deserves it more.'

Dylan's face brightened. 'Ah, Eoin, are you sure? That's really sound. You'll be first to come on if we need a sub.'

Eoin laughed. 'No, I'll be first on if you need a defender or midfielder. I'm not looking for any favours.'

'OK,' said a relieved Dylan. 'So then we have you, Sam, Jin Chen, Ronan and Andrew on the bench and that's our full squad sorted. I have to email it to the FAI tonight – for the programme – and McCaffrey wants the names of the starting eleven and subs too – he says he wants to let the past pupils know who is playing.'

CHAPTER 44

The final was set for Wednesday afternoon and for two days before it was all the boys could talk about. The first years were busy collecting autographs of the players and the junior dorms all had Rockets posters hanging out the windows.

'I wonder would Alan be able to do me up like a Panini sticker?' asked Dylan, in all seriousness, over breakfast on the morning of the game.

Eoin laughed. 'Don't forget, this is the last game the Red Rockets will ever play,' he told him. 'And it's back to rugby for me as soon as this is over.'

'Even the senior cup lads are talking about this game,' said Mikey.

'This is going to be huge,' said Dylan, 'Did you hear the games master's coach is already booked out? He says he's going to have to hire a second bus.'

'I hope Alan and a few of the others don't get overcome by the occasion,' said Eoin. 'We've played big games, finals, interpros, internationals. But Ferdia, Alan, James, they're all new to this sort of game. It can be a bit hard at first.'

'Yeah, do you remember that Fr Geoghegan Cup final in our first year in Castlerock?' asked Mikey. 'The crowd for the Leinster game kept coming in during our match – there must have been nearly thirty thousand watching the end of our game.'

'Yeah,' laughed Eoin, 'And they were all watching me taking the conversion for Shane's try!'

'Well that worked out well,' replied Dylan. 'And anyway, there won't be any Leinster – or Bohs – fans watching this time.'

The headmaster had given the football squad the morning off lessons so they spent the time relaxing and doing some light exercises. They had lunch at noon and after it was over they collected their kit bags and met outside the front of the school.

As they waited for Mr Finn and Mr Carey to arrive with the mini-bus, Mr McCaffrey came out of his office to talk to them. In his hand he was carrying a black plastic sack.

'Boys, I must confess I wasn't convinced of the merits of having an association football team in Castlerock College, where rugby has been our sporting choice for more than a hundred years,' the headmaster told them.

'However I have seen how you brought this squad together and shaped it into a unit and have been very impressed in the way you stuck to your task. To win two games in the competition from a standing start is an excellent performance and I am happy to admit I was wrong to place obstacles in your way.

'As a sign of how proud the school is of your achievements we would like to make a presentation to each of you.'

The headmaster lifted the black sack up onto the bench and produced a red shirt from the bag.

'Dylan Coonan,' he called out, and beckoned the captain to him.

'Here is the shirt you will wear today,' the head told him, 'It will look a lot better than that ragtag assortment of Arsenal and Liverpool shirts. I hope it brings you luck.'

Dylan took the bright red shirt off him and held it up to his team-mates. His name was across the back, and in the middle of the chest was the crest Alan had designed. Printed across the front in large letters was the name

'Castlerock Red Rockets.'

The boys each stepped up to receive their kit.

'Wow,' said Alan, as he collected his own shirt, 'just wow.'

Once the first eleven had received their tops, Mr McCaffrey reached into the bag and lifted out five more.

'And of course we have shirts for the substitutes,' he said, calling them up one by one as he read their names off the back.

'And finally we have...' he paused, looking puzzled. 'Madden. *Eoin* Madden? I thought he was injured.'

Eoin stepped forward. 'No sir, I was out for a few weeks, but I'm back training – I wouldn't be able to play a full game, but they might need me at some stage.'

Mr McCaffrey harrumphed. 'Well, make sure you're back for rugby anyway,' he told him.

Eoin thanked him, but he was irritated by the head-master's attitude.

'That's so petty,' he told Alan, under his breath. 'Gives with one hand and takes with the other.'

But Eoin soon forgot the slight when he joined the boys on the bus. And any fears about nerves were lost as Dylan led them all in a sing-song which won them plenty of attention when the bus stopped at traffic lights on its journey north towards Dalymount Park.

CHAPTER 45

hey arrived at the historic venue more than ninety minutes before kick-off. The boys who hadn't visited before were excited to be in the same dressing room as some of the greatest players of the past that they had heard their fathers talk about.

'I wonder where Seb Joyce sits?' wondered Alan.

The boys settled in and quickly put on their brand new shirts.

'They spelt my name wrong,' complained Charlie – 'It's Bermingham with an E, not Birmingham like the city in England.'

Dylan produced a marker pen and offered to make the necessary change but Charlie waved him away.

A knock came at the door and a man popped his head around the door. 'Welcome to Dalymount,' he said. 'I'm Luke, and here's a copy of the programme for each of you. Keep it safe, you'll want to remember this day seventy years from now.'

He went around the squad, giving each one of the players a programme and explaining where everything was in the ground and the timings they would have to follow. 'You can head out for a kickabout first, if you like,' he suggested.

The boys followed Luke out of the dressing room, up the tunnel, and out onto the beautiful green pitch.

'This is even better than one of Billy's surfaces' said Ferdia as he bent to touch the smooth grass.

'You've no chance of going over on your ankle like in my old school,' said Sam.

The boys did their stretches before heading off on a gently-paced lap of the pitch. Eoin spotted some of his team-mates looking up at the enormous terraces, perhaps wondering what they looked like when they were packed with supporters.

They came around the finishing straight in front of the stand and Eoin smiled as he remembered the photo hanging on the wall inside of dozens of fans standing on the roof trying to get a free view of an Ireland game against Italy. It reminded him of when they met Phil and Liam at the ground and he decided he would try to find the photo of the Manchester United team.

As soon as the warm-up was over, Eoin excused

himself and went for a wander around the corridors, and quickly found the photograph he was looking for.

He gazed at the group of young men, soon to be lost in a terrible plane crash. He found 'W. Whelan' in the back row and tapped the glass in front of his face.

'Hey, mind my nose,' came a voice from over Eoin's shoulder. He turned to find Liam grinning back at him.

'Hi, Liam,' replied Eoin. 'I was hoping we might see you today. We're playing a match here, it's a cup final with the school team.'

'Ah that's wonderful,' replied Liam. 'I'll let Phil know too – is his grandson playing?'

Eoin nodded, and quickly filled Liam in on the drama at the RDS.

'Those blaggards from Ballsbridge!' he said. 'They were only a junior club when I was playing, but they had a bad reputation. I see nothing has changed.'

'We're kicking off at half-past four so I better get back to the lads,' Eoin told him. 'It would be great if Phil was here – Alan's dad will be coming along too so it would great for them all to meet up.'

Eoin returned to the dressing room and sat down beside Alan, letting him know in a whisper about his encounter with Liam.

As Eoin had feared, Alan was starting to look very

nervous as kick-off time got closer. He tried to distract him by talking about a film they had seen over the summer, but it didn't work for very long.

'So dad *and* grandad are here watching. No pressure so,' he sighed.

'But you're wearing Phil's socks, so you will be fine,' replied Eoin.

Alan did relax a bit once he realised he had his lucky footwear, and by the time Dylan had a lengthy discussion about tactics it was soon time to go out to the pitch.

Luke knocked on the door again and told them the referee was waiting in the tunnel. The boys trooped out, Eoin nodding at the Ligouri boys who were also itching to get out to play.

'Ah, it's the "rebel soccer club",' said the Ligouri coach. 'Congratulations on your great run. I always knew you had a lot of talent. Good luck today.'

Dylan thanked him and after the linesmen checked the length of their studs, they trotted out onto the field.

CHAPTER 46

All Eoin's efforts to calm Alan's nerves collapsed when they heard an enormous roar from all around the stand. Both schools had brought a large number of supporters and almost all were on their feet, stamping and chanting about how great their team was.

Eoin looked up into the VIP box and spotted Mr Finn and Mr McCaffrey clapping them. He caught Mr Finn's eye and gave him a wave.

The team went about their pre-match routines, stretching muscles and warming up their kicking legs. Charlie threw himself about the goalmouth to give himself a feel of the football before the referee blew a long whistle and called the teams into the middle of the field.

The stadium PA crackled and Luke came on the microphone.

'Welcome everyone to Dalymount Park for the

Gillespie Cup final. Congratulations to both sides on qualifying for the final and we hope you have a memorable and enjoyable day here in the home of Irish football, no matter the result.

'We usually have a special guest along from the FAI to meet the teams, but today we have an extra special one. Once he heard that Castlerock Red Rockets were in the final he asked could he come along and meet the teams, and could he present the trophy.

'We couldn't say no to one of our greatest local heroes, even if he probably won't be here for very much longer. I'd like you to put your hands together and give a warm welcome to… Sebastian Joyce!'

The crowd gave a huge cheer. Almost everyone in the country now knew his name after hearing it many times in recent weeks discussed on TV and radio in the same breath as the great teams from Manchester, Liverpool, London and all over Europe.

Seb walked out onto the pitch, waving as the supporters cheered him all the way to the middle.

He shook hands with the Ligouri College team, and Dylan led him along the line, introducing the Red Rockets squad as he went. Eoin was at the very end of the line, and Seb perked up when he heard his name.

'Ah, Eoin Madden,' he said, with a large grin. 'I

certainly owe you a debt of gratitude, lad. Good luck today, and I hope we can meet up for a chat after the game.'

Eoin nodded, and when the referee blew the whistle again he trotted off to join his fellow substitutes on the bench.

'That was amazing,' said Jin Chen, 'he's a superstar – or he soon will be anyway.'

There was an even louder buzz around the ground as the ref blew the whistle to start the game.

'Come on Castlerock,' came a booming voice from the VIP box. Eoin looked over his shoulder and was astonished to see the headmaster was standing up bellowing his support.

It was a cagey opening half, with both teams finding it hard to get used to a pitch that was quite a bit bigger than the ones they were used to. Both defences were content to sit back and soak up the pressure, with few real chances created.

In the dressing room at half-time Ernesto was very frustrated. 'I have not had one ball passed to me,' he complained. 'We cannot win unless we have chances,' he added.

'It's hard for the midfield, though,' pointed out Figo. 'We have a huge amount of ground to cover and their defence is rock solid.'

'We're going to have to come up with something new,' said Dylan. 'Maybe Alan and Theo could push up more and try to catch them on the break. Ferdia could drop back to cover them.'

Once the chat was over, Eoin slipped away to use the bathroom. As happened several times before during a big game, Brian was there to meet him.

'I presume you don't have any soccer tips for me, Brian,' Eoin asked with a grin. 'Though as I'm sitting on the bench I don't really expect to have any chance to use them.'

'No, to be honest I'm just along for the ride,' Brian answered. 'I met Liam outside, he's expecting Phil to turn up at some stage. Will you get a game?'

'I doubt it,' replied Eoin, 'and to be honest I hope I don't. I'm a bit rusty – I've hardly played at all.'

CHAPTER 47

The second half sparked into life almost immediately, with Ligouri's captain charging upfield on a run from the tip-off, bouncing off a tackle from Paddy and crashing the ball off Charlie's right hand post.

The ball ricocheted away and Alan cleared it up to Richie.

'Phew, that could have been ugly,' Eoin told Ronan, who was sitting beside him on the bench.

'They must have had a pep talk from their coach,' he replied. 'I hope our guys listened to Dylan.'

Alan and Theo were indeed much more alert for chances to break from defence and the left-back made a run which only ended when he was fouled just outside the Ligouri area.

Figo stood over the ball and directed his team-mates to where they should make their runs. Dylan had urged Alan to come up the field in case of a rebound so he was hanging around the corner of the box when Figo took the free.

The ball flew hard and true towards the top corner, but Ligouri's goalkeeper got across and got his hand to the ball. It clipped off the post and landed at the feet of a defender who panicked and kicked it high in the air. Alan watched it fall and realised he would be closest to it when it landed, so he got in position to trap the ball. He managed to get his foot over the ball before it bounced and with one movement he turned and chipped the ball back towards the goal.

Ernesto had ghosted back in behind the defence and was waiting as the ball sailed over the keeper – and with a firm side-foot he ushered the ball into the back of the net.

The striker threw his arms into the air and his team-mates rushed to congratulate him. Eoin stood and looked back into the stands where he saw Alan's parents were also whooping with delight. He also noticed that Phil was standing behind them with a broad smile on his face, although it seemed that his son didn't yet know of his presence.

The goal spooked the Ligouri boys and they came charging back with wave after wave of attacks, but even when they got a shot off Charlie was there to keep them scoreless.

They couldn't keep up the pace and soon tired. Dylan brought on Ronan for James and Jin Chen for Cillian and their extra energy helped Castlerock keep things tight.

Eoin looked up at the stadium clock and reckoned there was about four minutes left to play. Ligouri were camped in the Rockets' half and won yet another corner when Charlie palmed the ball around the post.

'Everyone back!' roared Dylan, and Ernesto and Ronan dutifully trooped back into the box.

Their opponents played the corner short and moved out to improve the angle. The cross was swung in towards the back post where Alan headed it clear, but the ball was picked up again by the boys in blue and yellow. The Ligouri winger pushed the ball through a gap and their striker turned quickly and slammed the ball into the net.

The Red Rockets were stunned by the setback and Dylan tried hard to get them to lift their heads and start again. As they were waiting to kick off again, Alan asked the referee how long was left to play.

'Two minutes, lad,' he replied.

'And then extra time?' asked Alan.

'No,' answered the ref. 'It's straight to penos.'

Play resumed and Castlerock tried to create another

chance, but the stuffing had been knocked out of them.

'We're playing like we're already beaten,' Alan said to himself as the clock wound down. But he suddenly remembered something and dashed over to the referee at the next break in play.

'How long's left ref?' he called.

'Thirty-five seconds,' answered the match official.

'We want to make a substitution,' he said.

'What? With half-a-minute left? Are you mad?'

'No,' Alan replied, before he shouted to his team-mate – 'Ferdia, do you mind going off? We need to bring a sub on?'

Ferdia ran off while Alan shouted, 'Eoin, come on, we need you now.'

Eoin was a bit stunned, but he realised instantly what Alan was up to.

Play resumed and Eoin didn't get anywhere near the ball before the final whistle blew.

Dylan stormed up to Alan. 'What do you think you were doing with that messing at the end? We've half an hour extra time and Eoin's not fit enough for that.'

Alan smiled. 'I checked with the referee – there's no extra time. We're going straight the penalties and Eoin was as good a peno taker as anyone we have. I thought it was a good idea to bring him on.'

It slowly dawned on Dylan that Alan's brainwave was actually quite a brilliant one – or at least it would be if Eoin scored of course.

CHAPTER 48

The teams lined up on the half-way line and faced the Schoolhouse End where the penalty shoot-out would take place.

Castlerock's quintet was made up of the four who had scored twice out of two kicks in the competition back at school – Richie, Ernesto, Alan and Eoin – while Dylan decided he would lead from the front by taking the first kick himself.

Eoin watched as Ligouri started with a successful kick and Dylan slammed home the first goal for the Rockets. But he then decided he couldn't watch any more until his own time came, and he turned and faced the goal at the other end of the ground.

'Howya Eoin,' came a familiar voice. 'Have you an attack of nerves?'

'Nah, not quite,' replied Eoin. 'I just don't enjoy these shootouts, I'll just wait for my own and do what I have to do.'

'There were no penalty shoot outs in my day,' said Liam, 'but I used to love taking penos. I was top scorer the year we won the league and I got a few from the spot.

'The trick is to let the keeper see you look at *both* posts and pick a spot inside both of them,' he added. 'That should make him confused – but then you never look at them again. Decide which one of them you're going for and hit the ball low and hard. Don't change your mind. Nineteen times out of twenty the keeper won't get down in time.'

Eoin heard a couple of cheers, but couldn't work out what they meant for the scoreline.

'I scored two goals against Shamrock Rovers in that European Cup match here,' recalled Liam, who went on to show Eoin exactly how and where he scored them from.

The crowd continued to roar at short intervals, but Eoin was only dragged away from Liam's stories by a shout from Alan.

'Come on, Eoin, you're up next,' he called.

Eoin trotted up just in time to see Charlie make a fingertip save from the Ligouri star midfielder.

'What's the score?' he asked his pal, above the cheers

from Castlerock supporters.

'Are you serious?' replied Alan. 'Were you not watching? It's four-four, but we have one kick left. If you get it we win!'

Eoin walked towards the goal and picked up the ball, rolling it around in his hands. He placed it precisely on the spot and took five steps backwards. He chuckled to himself how he better not get confused and try to put it over the bar, like in rugby.

But his mind instantly raced back to the job in hand.

'Here we go,' he said to himself. 'My first ever kick of a ball in a competitive football match and I could win the cup for the school.'

He flicked his eyes from one goalpost to another, plotting in his mind that he would aim inside the left post. He ran up slowly, lifted his right leg, and drilled the ball low and hard towards the bottom corner. The keeper guessed correctly, but the shot was fast enough to beat his dive and the net rippled upwards as the ball nestled in it.

'Yessssss!' roared Dylan, punching the air as he raced towards Eoin. Within seconds the scorer was buried in a mound of players, soon to be joined by the substitutes too. Once the ruck had broken up Eoin went over to shake the hand of the Ligouri goalkeeper, and as many of their players as he could find.

Out came an FAI official with the trophy and placed it on a stand. The PA kicked into life and Luke came on to tell them that the presentation would now take place and that the special guest had stayed around to hand out the medals.

The losing side collected theirs first, and the Castlerock boys clapped and cheered their opponents. Then Dylan called out the names of his team-mates and Seb Joyce put the gold medals around each of their necks.

'That was a very exciting game,' Seb told the crowd. 'There was a lot of skill and talent on display and I hope you all continue playing soccer and your school continues to enter this excellent competition. And now I am greatly honoured to present the Gillespie Cup to Dylan Coonan, captain of the Castlerock Red Rockets!'

Dylan lifted the silver cup high over his head and turned to face the stand as hundreds of mobile phone cameras captured the moment in a click. Eoin noticed that there were five or six teachers present from the school and the biggest grin of all was on the face of the headmaster.

CHAPTER 49

Back in the dressing room the boys continued to chant and sing as they passed the cup around and posed for photos. Mr McCaffrey came down to visit and told them they had no homework for three nights. This was greeted with laughter as the boys in Transition Year had no homework anyway.

'I must say your red shirts looked very well,' he added, 'and the school is very proud of your performance and the manner of your victory.'

Eoin grinned at Alan, 'One kick of the ball and I win the cup. I like this soccer thing.'

'It was a pretty tasty kick, to be fair,' said Alan.

'Yeah, I got a bit of last-minute coaching from a man well used to scoring here. It was more than sixty years ago but he knows what's talking about.'

Alan laughed. 'Was Liam there on the pitch with you? I thought you were talking to yourself. Any sign of my grandad?'

'Yes – did you not see him? When you set up that goal for Ernesto I spotted him in the crowd, he was standing right behind your folks. I don't think they knew he was there.'

Alan smiled. 'I must go and check if they're still around…'

Luke popped his head inside the door to tell them that the bar was now open and was serving soft drinks and snacks for the teams and their parents and teachers.

'Perfect,' said Alan, 'I'll see if Mum and Dad will come in.'

Eoin finished getting changed and packed his bag away. He would ring Dixie and his parents to tell them they had won – he had decided not to tell them about the final as he didn't expect to play and they lived more than a hundred miles away.

There was a nice buzz in the bar and even the Ligouri boys seemed to have got over the defeat. Eoin chatted to a couple of them before he was called aside by Luke.

'Seb wants a word with you,' he told him. 'He doesn't want to come in here – he hates being mobbed – so he asked could you go out the back door of the bar, he'll see you in the foyer beside the old photos.'

'Can I bring Alan and Dylan? They're huge Bohs fans,'

asked Eoin, and Luke nodded.

The boys slipped out of the bar to meet their hero. Eoin introduced Seb to his friends.

'You're the lad with those funny old Bohs socks,' he told Alan. 'Alfie pointed them out to me when we were watching the game. He recognised them as the style back in the sixties.'

Alan told them they were worn by his grandfather who was also a Dalymount Park legend.

Seb handed Eoin a bag, saying, 'Thanks again for saving my ankle. You don't know just how much that could have ruined my life.'

Eoin peeked inside, and saw the bag contained a Bohemians shirt and a training jacket.

'I won't be needing these for much longer,' Seb said, with a wink. 'You have to promise me you won't tell anyone what I'm going to say next.'

The boys nodded.

'OK, well I suppose you've heard about all sorts of clubs looking for me to join them. I've never wanted to leave Bohs, but the money they're going to make will transform this place, and hopefully help them buy better players and win more trophies.

'I've decided to go to the club that gave Bohs the best deal, not just the most money. And one of them promised to come over and play a friendly here every pre-season for five years. You'll probably read all about it in the papers in a day or two, but from now on I'm going to play for Manchester United.'

'Yesssss,' said Dylan, punching the air for the second time in less than an hour.

'That's a great choice, son,' came another voice, causing Seb to turn around.

Standing in front of him was Liam, wearing the same United kit he had worn in the same ground more than sixty years before.

Seb was puzzled. 'Sorry, who are you? That's some seriously vintage United shirt.'

Liam turned to Eoin. 'I think you better explain,' he said.

Eoin told Seb the basic story of how he can see ghosts and when he first met Liam in this very spot.

'I thought I recognised you,' said a stunned Seb. 'I live near where you're from over in Cabra. There's a plaque to you on the railway bridge over there. You're a real hero to people from around there.'

'Ah, thanks for saying that,' replied Liam, 'But I was just a footballer, I wasn't a hero.

'And what did you think of the Red Rockets?' asked Seb.

'They're not bad at all for a team that have only started,' said Liam. 'There's three or four who have a real bit of talent and I hope they stick with it.'

'I agree,' said Seb. 'That Ernesto lad is class, and Duffy, the Number Seven, has a lovely touch. And that lad who took the last peno has some rocket of a shot.'

Eoin grinned. 'What did you think of Alan – not just his socks?'

'Ah, he's good enough, he got a couple of lovely crosses in,' replied Seb.

'I'm not surprised at all, he's got football blood running through his veins,' said Phil who had just appeared in the doorway. 'I've been trying to tell his father that,' he added, as Alan's parents walked into the foyer.

'Hey, Dylan,' said Eoin as he gestured at the room now starting to fill up, 'I think it's time to head back to school. You'll be OK here Alan, I'm sure your dad will drop you back. It looks like you all have quite a lot to talk about.'

ALSO AVAILABLE

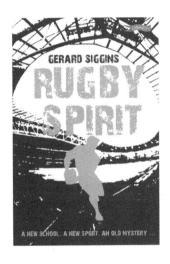

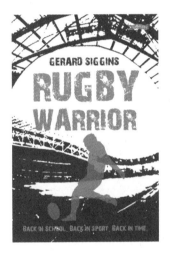

Eoin has just started a new school … and a new sport. Everyone at school is mad about rugby, but Eoin hasn't even held a rugby ball before! And why does everybody seem to know more about his own grandad than he does?

Eoin Madden is now captain of the Under 14s team and has to deal with friction between his friend Rory and new boy Dylan as they battle for a place as scrum-half. Fast-paced action, mysterious spirits and feuding friends – it's a season to remember!

GERARD SIGGINS

RUGBY REBEL

DISCOVERING HISTORY, UNCOVERING MYSTERY

GERARD SIGGINS

RUGBY RUNNER

ANCIENT ROOTS, MODERN BOOTS

What's the link between Eoin's history lessons and the new spirit he's spotted wearing a Belvedere rugby jersey? … Historical and modern mysteries combine in this intriguing tale of rugby, rebellion and ghosts.

Eoin is captain of the Junior Cup team, training with Leinster and aiming for Ireland's Under 16 World Cup team. He also has to deal with a ghost on a mission that goes back to the very origins of the game of rugby.

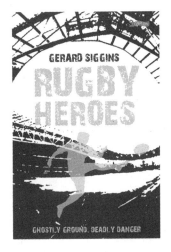

Eoin has been chosen for the Junior development squad so over the summer he gets to go to Dublin for a rugby summer school. But when his new friends are taken on a trip to Twickenham, London, to play & watch rugby there are ghostly goings on..

Eoin been called up for Ireland in the Under 16 Four Nations!
When his oldest and best ghostly friend calls for help, can Eoin and his band of heroes solve their deadliest mystery yet

With no rugby over the summer, Eoin and his friends head to Ormondstown GAA club to get involved in hurling and football. Some local bullies spoil things a bit – but when the ghosts of Brian Hanrahan and Michael Hogan appear, it's clear there is something more sinister brewing..